Truck Drivin' Man: Warrior of the Road

Donna M. Bryan

Copyright © 2011 Donna M. Bryan

This is a book of fiction. Names, characters, and incidents are products of the author's imagination. Any resemblance to actual events, locales, or persons living or dead, is entirely coincidental.

All rights reserved.

ISBN: 146366866X
ISBN-13: 978-1463668662

DEDICATION

This book is dedicated to my children who have encouraged me to write down my stories.

I also want to acknowledge the wonderful assistance of those in my writer's group for their critiquing.

Thank you very much!

CAST OF CHARACTERS

Main Characters

Jack O'Ryan	Semi Truck Driver
Bob and Alice O'Ryan	Jack's parents
Daniel O'Ryan	Jack's brother
Deb Kramer	Jack's sister Joe
Kramer	Brother-in-law
Katie Kramer	Niece
Mira Kramer	Niece
Rosie	Friend
Carl	Rosie's business partner
Sara Taylor	Friend
Brian Taylor	Sara's son
Jimmy Taylor	Sara's deceased husband
Mike Kincaid	Friend
Mary and Calvin Kincaid	Mike's parents
Kevin Kincaid	Mike's brother
Pierre and Annette Goncourt	Canadian friends
Louisa Goncourt	Daughter
Lou	Trucker Friend
Jason Johnson	Lou's son
Carol	Pregnant unmarried waitress

Bayou Friends

Granny	Head of clan
Contessa	Granddaughter
Rafe	Grandson
Cray	Nephew
Manny	Nephew
Auntie Kate	Healer/Spiritual, Cajun and regular religion

INTRODUCTION

'Truck Drivin' Man' is a story of Jack, a semi driver. A semi driver must like his own company, since he spends the majority of his life alone in the truck. The truck is more than an eighteen wheeler; it's his home away from home, his livelihood, his friend and his enemy. He must have a CDL, which is a commercial driving license. All drivers are required to keep a log which tells how many miles and hours they have driven, and how many stops they have made. Under the law, they have fourteen hours work time, they can drive eleven hours and then they must stop for ten hours. Failure to do so will result in large fines.

The driver is responsible for his truck and the merchandise he is transporting. If it's a reefer (refrigerated truck) there are extra tasks to constantly do. He has appointments to make, managers, dispatchers, and receptionists to deal with if he is late. He must be alert to all types of traffic situations in strange locations. Sometimes he must use the truck routes through a town.

He must have the knowledge to do small repairs until he can reach a truck garage or have the repair service come to him. This is frustrating. Drivers get paid by the hub mile, or as the wheel rolls. Downtime means expenses but no income.

Some places have *lumpers*. These are men who get paid to unload the trucks. They will charge the drivers extra, if they can get away with it. If the drivers don't pay them, their trailer may sit until the product is needed or their truck will be the last one unloaded.

These hearty drivers brave all types of weather conditions and terrain, from winding, steep mountain roads, to windy, monotonous stretches of flat land. They put on snow chains in biting cold weather and sweat when the air-conditioner goes out.

They must always be on the alert for sleepy, drunk, or dangerous drivers, low overheads and the constant scrutiny of the D.O.T. (Department of Transportation) whenever the 'open' sign is on. Drivers must pull in if the sign or light is on.

Thank goodness there are truck stops with twenty-four hour service for these warriors of the road. Showers, washers/dryers, phones, good food, audio/video rentals and some even have small chapels. We take having a daily shower for granted. Drivers can't always get one. Many of the tired truckers have a hard time finding a place to park and shut down for the night.

Yes, it's a lonely job, one that requires many talents and long hours away from family. These are the men and women who keep commerce going, by transporting various products.

This story is of Jack's life as a trucker, driving back and forth across the United States and up into Canada.

CHAPTER 1

"You're positive about taking off in this terrible weather?" Rosie leaned against the table as she set the full thermos of coffee in front of Jack. "There's some talk about shutting down the road." She looked concerned. She liked this regular customer, if you could call his stopping in about once a month regular.

Glancing at the pouring rain, Jack let out a huge sigh. He had pushed hard to get here on time and now the company said they needed the remainder of the load dropped off in Santa Fe, the sooner the better. He slid out of the booth and reached for the bill. "Don't worry that pretty red head of yours, Rosie. You know I'm the best trucker on the road." He gave a low chuckle and patted her shoulder.

She shook her shoulder length reddish blond hair. "You truckers are all the same, thinking you're in a league with Superman." Together they walked toward the cashier. "But silly me, I keep forgetting you're a professional truck driver, and modest too." Rosie leaned against the counter, crossed her arms in front of her green uniform, and with a warm smile, looked up at him, all six feet two inches without his boots on.

For over a year, Jack had been stopping here whenever he had a load to deliver in the area. Unlike some drivers, he was always clean, both his clothes and his language. Rosie liked that in a man. She gave him a discreet glance, appraising him. She had to admit, he looked pretty darn good in those jeans.

Today he was wearing a dark blue western shirt with pearl buttons. His well worn boots had been polished many a time, and the soles replaced. Somehow he always managed to have a nice hair cut. Jack didn't go around all shaggy and greasy. Yeah, he was a woman's kind of man. Well, at least her kind of man.

After Jack shrugged into his raincoat, Rosie handed him the thermos of coffee he had ordered.

"Take care, Jack. Leave your radio on for the weather report. The roads get pretty dangerous when it's been raining as long and hard as it has been the last two days. The conditions are right for mud slides and flash flooding. We don't want to lose a good customer, especially one who always leaves a 'healthy' tip." Rosie grinned at him. She stood with her hands on her hips and a friendly smile on her face. No one would know she was half owner of this busy truck stop.

Jack placed his hat firmly on his head, and cradling the thermos in his left arm, answered, "And here I thought it was just my good looks and wonderful personality you liked." They both laughed as he headed for the door.

Just as Jack reached for the door, three armed men wearing black masks burst through the entry way, knocking Jack to the floor with a thud, his western hat flying across the floor. The thermos rolled over to rest by Rosie's feet, but in the excitement, nobody noticed.

A waitress screamed and dropped a food laden tray, causing the customers to look at the source of the crash.

"Don't anybody move!" shouted one of the robbers, a tall man wearing a blue coat with a red bandana covering his face as he pointed his gun at Jack.

Jack stayed on the floor as told. He didn't want to rile this man unnecessarily. He hoped everyone else would stay calm, not panic. Mentally, Jack was assessing the dangerous situation. He had to do something he couldn't just lay here like a sack of potatoes. There wasn't any guarantee the robbers wouldn't shoot them anyway.

Jack knew a couple of drivers would be coming from the showers soon. He hoped they would notice the absence of restaurant noises and check things out, not barge into the room and get hurt. He was counting on them to help somehow if possible.

The short man waved his rifle back and forth at the other frightened customers, while the third man went in the direction of the kitchen. Soon the white faced kitchen crew stumbled into the dining room with the armed heavy set man behind them, pushing at them with his gun and acting cocky. "Look what I found hiding in the pantry."

"Shut up!" the tall man ordered. "We're here to get the money, not talk." Throwing a rolled up pillow case at Rosie, he growled, "Where's the safe, and don't tell me you ain't got one!"

Rosie's face blanched as she slowly bent over and picked up the pillow case, her eyes never leaving the gun. "It's… it's in the office, but I… I don't have the combination. Ca-Carl has it, and, and he… he just left for the bank." Her voice trembled.

With all eyes on Rosie, Jack slowly reached into his jacket and quietly turned on his cell phone and hit the buttons 9-1-1, hoping the dispatcher could hear the robbery going on. Jack surmised that Carl was really in the office, and assuming he heard the commotion through the closed door, called the police.

Little by little, without being observed, Jack slowly pushed himself in a sitting position. He had to be ready to rush the thieves if the opportunity arose.

"Don't give me any of that hogwash, little lady. I wasn't born yesterday. I know you keep money around. Move. Now!" The hard stare of the brown eyes looking over the mask showed he meant business.

Rosie's feet felt like lead as she slowly walked toward the office, hoping that Carl was aware of the robbery. Her heart was beating furiously as she stopped at the closed door.

"Open it lady. I ain't got all day," the tall man snarled as he roughly pushed her against the door.

Jack's blood pressure soared when he saw Rosie lurch forward by the force of the shove, and he moved.

"Mister, I thought you were told to stay put. If I see so much as a hair on your head wiggle, so help me, I'm going to shoot you. Do you hear me?" The short man tapped the barrel of the gun on Jack's shoulder.

Without thinking, Jack grabbed the barrel with both hands, causing the man to fall forward with a grunt. Kicking the rifle out of range, Jack leaped on top of him as a trooper came charging in.

With his drawn revolver pointed at the other robber, the trooper growled, "Don't move," He waved for his back up to come in.

They had traced Jack's call and heard the background sounds of the robbery in progress.

Cool-headed Carl had hidden behind the door and clobbered the robber on the head with a lamp as he came through the office doorway, causing the gun to discharge a bullet that grazed Rosie's arm, before it hit the wall.

When Jack heard the shot ring out from the office, and Rosie's scream, his stomach muscles contracted at the sound.

"Rosie!" Jack yelled out as he sprinted for the room, his heart pumping with fear of what he might find.

Through the open door, Jack saw the heavy set man sprawled out on the floor. Kneeling, Jack gathered Rosie in his arms. "Are you okay? Hurt?" He pulled back to look at her, and saw blood on her blouse sleeve. "Let me check your arm!"

Rosie shook her head no, and leaned back into his arms. She was still frightened and Jack felt so safe and secure.

They remained that way; Jack getting his heart beat back to normal, Rosie taking comfort from his touch, as they watched the activity in the room.

Jack got put his arm around her and led Rosie out to the dining room where an Emergency Medical Tech checked her arm. She had a good scrape, one that bled a lot, but nothing really serious. One of the EMT's bandaged the wound and inquired if her tetanus shot was up to date. Receiving the affirmative, they left.

More policemen entered the office and took over with the investigation. The three men were unmasked, handcuffed, read their rights, and taken out to the squad car. The police began to question the witnesses.

Carl went over to Rosie and squatted down by her chair. "Rosie, what say we give out some free coffee and pastries to the people while the police finish their questioning? I think it might relax everyone."

"Sure, fine," Rosie rubbed her hand across her hair, "I... I'll get right to it," and slowly started to rise from the chair.

"Oh no you don't my friend, you're done for the day, Rosie. Relax and rest your arm." Carl's voice was firm but friendly.

"I agree," Jack chimed in giving Carl a nod that he approved of the decision.

Jack went over to the counter and requested two cups of hot tea, and carried them back to the table where Rosie sat.

"My mom always says a nice cup of tea makes things better," Jack said placing the cups on the table.

Jack was relieved to see her color coming back to normal and her body relaxing.

"Some entertainment you provide. All I wanted was a meal and coffee to go, I really didn't have time for a cops and robbers program." Jack placed his hand over hers.

"I couldn't believe how frightened I was, Jack. I've always prided myself on being strong, and I just froze and stuttered." Rosie leaned back against the chair.

"Don't be so hard on yourself, Rosie. It's not like they came in and we had a dress rehearsal." (*Now why did I say something stupid like that?*) Jack mentally kicked himself.

But it struck Rosie as funny, and she started to smile, then laugh out loud. "I can just see a comedy routine; **The Three Stoodges** dressed up like policemen, the robbers dropping their guns, and the waitresses going in one door and out the other."

"And then they reverse, and everyone is chasing the policemen." Jack joined in with the fantasy.

The laugh relaxed Rosie for a minute, then with a somber look at Jack, "We can kid about it now, but Jack, I'm so glad you were here. I can't thank you enough for your concern."

"When that jerk pushed you, I was ready to tackle him and teach him some manners. Having a rifle barrel pointed at my head changed my priorities until that gun went off! I felt scared. I didn't want you injured."

Rosie leaned her head on his shoulder. "Things could have turned out differently. It's fortunate no one got hurt." She giggled, "I think one robber is going to have a very throbbing headache for awhile though."

Jack smiled. "I just wish it would have been me instead of Carl that bonked him over the head," he glanced up at the clock. "I hate to leave, Rosie, but I know you are okay and I really need to get on the road and just deal with careless drivers and such. I think I've had enough excitement for one day."

Jack stood up and Rosie did too. Jack hugged her for a long moment. Um, she felt so warm in his arms. Sighing, he stepped back and smiled at her.

Leaning down he picked up his thermos, shook it, not hearing anything broken, he headed for the door. Looking through the glass door and not seeing any other unwanted characters outside; he turned, and waved good-by. He was going to miss her.

CHAPTER 2

Opening the door, Jack lowered his head against the blowing wind and stinging rain that lashed at him. Taking long strides he tried to avoid puddles of water as he hurried to the semi. Quickly unlocking the door, he stepped up into the cab leaving a trail of water on the rubber mat. Setting the thermos in the holder, he removed his hat and rain jacket and hung them on the hook behind the seat. Jack sighed, "It's going to be a very long night."

Jack had let the truck idle while he was eating. He quickly went through his checklist, and looked over his driving log. You never knew when the Department Of Transportation boys would be out, although Jack couldn't imagine any of the weigh stations being open in this storm. "Well, everything checks out. No use sitting here, when I've plenty of miles to put on," Jack said out loud.

As he put the truck into gear and pulled out of the parking spot, he looked back at the lights of the truck stop through his side mirrors, and thought of that cute waitress, Rosie. "Maybe if I had someone like her at home, I wouldn't be driving on a wet night like this, alone…" Jack muttered to himself.

The traffic was light, not many trucks on the road. That was okay with Jack. His CB was on and Jack could hear the other drivers talking about getting off the road and shutting down until the rain became a slow drizzle or stopped.

Jack mentally kicked himself, "I should have stayed at the truck stop where at least I had some company." The rain sounded like small bullets hitting the truck windshield. The wipers were working at full capacity and didn't succeed in keeping the windows clear. He couldn't just stop in the road; someone would ram into the back of the semi, or under it. He kept a tight grip on the steering wheel

Slowing his speed way down, Jack used the highway markers to keep on the road. At the next turn-off he would find a safe spot to park then crawl into his bunk and sleep a few hours until it quit storming.

He was relieved that Sacramento exit wasn't too far away. The strain and tension of driving in this downpour was exhausting. His eyes felt like they were squeezed in a tight fist from the strain of looking through the blurred windshield.

Then a trucker's worst nightmare happened. The rapidly falling rain produced a sudden avalanche of water and thick mud sliding down the mountain side and across the road. Instantly, the water was hub high on the wheels of the truck, and rapidly getting deeper. Jack looked out the right window but couldn't see a thing. He felt fear grip him. Beads of sweat appeared on his forehead. What should he do? There weren't really any options. Stop and let the force of mud and rain stall him, perhaps the power of the rushing gooey mess push him off the road and...the thought of being in the truck flipping over and over crashing down the mountain wasn't pretty.

"God, guide me through this," Jack cried out and gripping the steering wheel firmly in his hands, fighting to keep the semi on the liquid road, kept driving. Sweat poured in rivulets down his face and under his arms. What seemed like an eternity of driving was actually about a thousand feet and Jack was out of mud slide danger. Breathing a sigh of relief, Jack stopped the big rig and thanked God. Resting his head on the big steering wheel, Jack let his heartbeat slow down, and his legs quit feeling like rubber. He realized how close he had come to being seriously injured or killed if the rain and mud had pushed him off the road, down the steep mountain. He doubted if he and the truck would ever have been found.

Taking a deep breath, Jack continued on his way, and soon saw the mile marker indicating the next exit to be about a mile away. That would be the place to stop and wait out the storm. The sign appeared and he put on the turn signal even though there was no one behind him to see. It was an unconscious force of habit. He was almost to the stop sign when his headlights picked up a car half off the road, almost in the ditch. Swerving to the left, he observed someone in it. He pulled ahead of the car and stopped the truck.

"I'll call a wrecker, but first, I want to make sure no one in the car needs immediate assistance," Jack thought as he put on his rain slicker and hat. He paused to pick up the five cell flashlight and bracing himself, pushed open the door and stepped out, braving the harsh wind and driving rain. He was leery of walking up to a strange vehicle at night. You never knew when it could be a dangerous situation.

Flashing his light in the window of the driver's side, he saw a very frightened face looking back at him. A woman huddled in the middle of the seat, her arms holding a little boy, in a very protective manner.

"Are you okay?" Jack yelled through the window. "That's my truck up there." He pointed at it. "I can call for a wrecker, or have you already called for one?"

The young lady shook her head no and put her hand to her ear like a phone. She released her tight hold on the child enough so she could lean over and rolled the window down a little bit. She didn't know this guy from Adam, but she needed some help and hoped this stranger was the answer to her many prayers that day.

"My car just stopped without any warning and it seems like we've been here forever. You're the first person to stop and see if we needed any help. I would appreciate it if you did call the wrecker. You wouldn't happen to have an apple or some water that my son, Brian could have would you? He hasn't had anything to eat since this afternoon. He was sleeping and I didn't want to stop. I kept driving and then the car died..." Her voice trailed off. She couldn't understand why she was babbling so to a stranger. The fact was she needed help and hoped this man wasn't thief or worse.

The little boy in her arms looked up at Jack. His big brown eyes were trusting, yet questioned who Jack was, and why he and his mommy were sitting in the cold dark car in the rain.

Without thinking, Jack said, "Why don't you wrap a blanket around you and the boy and come back to my truck. I have some snacks in there, and you can use my phone to call your family and I'll call a wrecker. You can wait in my truck until it comes. At least you two won't be in the dark, and the heater works." The rain was cascading off his hat and splashing on the window.

Sara looked into his blue eyes. Her gut reaction said he was earnest. Maybe God directed this trucker *to answer* her prayer. The car was chilly. She shivered and wrapped the blanket tight around Brian.

Jack opened the door and reached for the little guy. Sara scrambled out fast and followed him to the huge truck. The cold rain pelted against her hunched body as she waited for Jack to unlock the passenger side door. Jack set the child inside, then turned to assist her into the cab. The steps were high, and she appreciated the help to climb up.

"I'll be just a minute," Jack shouted. "I need to set out the emergency triangles. We don't want anyone running into your car." He shut the door firmly.

Sara jumped at the sound. What was she doing in the middle of the night in a stranger's truck? He could be a crazy nut. No...she had looked into his eyes; they would be safe with him.

Pulling the reflective triangles from the back of the semi, Jack set out the signs behind her vehicle. Then he locked the doors on her car before heading for the comfort of the warm truck.

The storm didn't show any signs of abating as Jack climbed into the cab, his slicker once again dripping water all over. As a matter of fact, the lightning lit up the sky and the thunder boomed loudly, startling all three of them.

Jack smiled at them as he took off his wet hat. "I guess the angels are bowling up in heaven tonight."

"Sounded like a strike to me." Sara replied with a nervous laugh.

The two looked at him with big eyes, not sure what to do next.

Sara quickly glanced around the inside of the cab. She had never been in a truck like this one before and was surprised at how roomy it was. In her wildest dreams she couldn't imagine driving anything this huge. Her parking wasn't the greatest with her much smaller Buick.

Jack took off his wet slicker and hung it up with the soggy hat. Turning around, "Hey, little fellow, let's get that wet blanket off you." He reached for the quiet little boy. Brian never hesitated, but raised his little arms up to Jack. Jack took the wet blanket off the young lad and set him down on the lower bunk.

He turned around and saw Sara shivering in the passenger seat, her arms wrapped around herself, observing his every move. She was cold, wet, and unsure of her situation. Jack felt sorry for her.

"Let me put a call through for help, and then I'll find something dry you can put on," Jack said as he slipped into his seat and reached for the cell phone. He contacted the state patrol, gave their location and requested a wrecker. The officer responded that due to the road conditions, everyone was staying put unless there was an injury. Jack assured him no one was hurt.

Sara looked at Jack wondering, *"Now what?"*

Jack handed her the phone. "Call anyone you need to and let them know you're okay. Ah, by the way, what's your name?"

"Sara, and this is my son Brian." She shook her head. "Like I told you, there really isn't anyone to call."

Jack didn't know what to make of that, but he didn't push the subject. It wasn't any of his business, and she didn't have the appearance of a lady gangster. He looked at her, wet and shivering, and thought he better get her some dry clothes to put on. Then he would check to see what he had left of fruit and other snacks to feed them. "I know we're strangers, but you can trust me. You need to change into something dry. I'll pull the curtain that separates the seats from my bunk area and you can pick out something of mine to put on until your clothes dry or it quits raining and you can get your suitcase. Are you comfortable with that?"

Sara nodded her head yes. It wasn't like she had other options available. Her wet hair was plastered to her face and her eyes big with questions.

Jack stood up and reached out his hand and she took it, then stepped back to the bunk where her son was sitting still, just looking at them. Jack took out a towel from one of the many cubby holes and handed it to her and pointed out where his clothes were. "Help yourself." Always the gentleman, he stepped back and closed the curtain.

Sitting in the driver's seat, Jack poured a cup of hot steaming coffee. He could hear the rustling of clothes as Sara changed into something warm and the murmur of voices as she reassured her son that everything was okay. Then Sara opened the curtain.

Jack almost laughed out loud and it took all he had to control it. She looked like a little waif. His brown flannel shirt was buttoned up to her neck. The sleeves were rolled up a couple of times and the tails of the shirt hung down to her knees. A pair of his gray boot socks covered her knees and she had a towel wrapped around her long wet hair.

Sara observed Jack trying to suppress laughing. His lips were twitching and his eyes full of merriment. "I take it from the look on your face, in this ensemble I won't make model of the year."

That did it! Jack couldn't hold back the laughter any longer and it burst forth from him in a torrent.

"Not even in the *Trucker's Gazette*."

Sara joined in the laughter and posed like a model.

"Mommy, I'm hungry." Brian had slipped off the bunk and was pulling on the tail of the shirt his mom was wearing. She picked him up and gave him a kiss on the cheek and glanced over at Jack.

Jack handed her the cup of hot coffee. "Why don't you both sit on the bunk so I have some room and I'll see what I can rustle up to eat. We can't have Brian starving."

Jack seemed to fill up the extra space as he moved back by them. There fitting in the space the size of a cooler, was a small refrigerator. Jack bent down, opened it and said, "Let's see, there's yogurt, cheese, apples, and a couple small boxes of soy milk." He stood up and reached into another cubby hole and brought out some crackers, bananas, spoons and paper towels.

Sara shook her head in amazement. Here it was, a little after midnight, and they were having a splendid picnic in a stranger's truck. This was a wonderful steel oasis in the midst of a terrible storm.

Jack had eaten at the truck stop and wasn't hungry. Pouring himself a cup of coffee, he watched the little guy eating away, not making a mess. Jack found that amazing. Most little kids had food all over. While the two ate, Jack began asking questions. "Sara, what brought you to this part of the state?" He took a sip of the steaming coffee.

"A change. My husband was killed in a work accident a year ago. I needed to get away from all the memories. I thought finding a new place to live, maybe going back to school part-time until Brian is in school all day, would chase away the sadness of losing Jim. I was driving to check out some different areas and then this happened." She took a sip of the coffee, raised her cup in a salute to him. "Good coffee."

Jack nodded in acknowledgement, "What about your family? Won't they be worried about you and your son? I'm sorry; I shouldn't be asking you these things. It's really none of my business." Gee, when had he turned into such a busy body?

"No, it's okay." Sara gave a deep sigh. "I was raised in a

foster home. They were good people. They came into my life at a badly needed time. My parents were alcoholics. My teacher noticed how unkempt and hungry I came to school and had the situation checked on. End result, I became a ward of the state."

Sara gathered up the napkins and remains from their nutritious snack. "I worked summers while I was in high school, and then I entered a junior college. Once you reach eighteen, you're on your own as far as the social system goes. I got a job and went to school. I had a nice efficiency apartment and life was going along fine. I felt real good about myself. Then I met Jimmy in one of the classes, and it was love at first sight." She looked at Jack, wondering if he was bored and she should stop.

"Go on," Jack prompted gently as if he had read her mind.

Brian crawled into his mother's lap and she cuddled him. "We dated for about six months and then Jimmy asked me to marry him. I was in seventh heaven. I loved him and his parents. They were good people and became the parents I never had. We were married in their back yard by the pastor of the church. It was a small wedding, but a beautiful one. It was the happiest day of my life."

Her voice trailed off and Jack could see that she was back to that happier time.

Returning back to the present, she continued, "Jimmy went to work full time and started to take night classes. I kept on working and going to classes too. Then I became pregnant with Brian. Jimmy and his parents felt I should quit my job and just go to school. Brian was due in the summer. After he was born, I didn't go back to school. I was so happy being a wife, mother, and keeping our home clean." A tear formed and started to roll down her cheek. She brushed it away.

Sara let out a huge sigh. "Then, the terrible day came when I got the call to go to the hospital. Jimmy had been hurt at work. But I got there too late. I really think he was dead before he arrived there. A piece of equipment failed and he was crushed to death. Part of me died that day with him. I don't think I could have gone on if it hadn't been for my little Brian.

He looks just like his Daddy." She kissed the top of her son's head. Sara sniffed and Jack handed her a tissue.

"What about your husband's folks? Didn't they help?" Jack wondered aloud.

"Oh, they were great! They wanted me to move in with them. They owned a big beautiful home," Sara hurriedly explained. "But, I wanted to stay in my home, where Jimmy, Brian, and I had been a happy family. I think they understood."

"Won't they be concerned now with you away from them, not knowing where you and their only grandson are?" Jack knew how he would feel. Upset.

"I lost them too, just six months ago. They were on vacation. Both of them were retired and they would take little mini trips. While on one of their trips, they were killed by a drunken driver." Sara started to sob, her shoulders shaking.

"Mommy, Mommy, don't cry." Brian sat up and put his little arms around his mother's neck. The little boy was visibly upset.

"Now I've done it," thought Jack to himself. "I couldn't leave well enough alone, just give them a place to rest and something to eat. Oh no. I had to open up a big bag of hurtful memories. Now he had her crying and the little boy upset too. He wasn't good at handling tears. Changing tires maybe, but not wiping tears."

He reached over and gently touched her arm, "Sara, I am truly sorry for your losses. I never should have asked you all those questions. I didn't mean to pry and make you cry."

She smiled through her tears as he handed her another tissue and she blew her nose. "No, I needed this. I've held in the hurt for such a long time. Maybe you should hang out your shingle and become Doctor...by the way, what is your name?"

"Jack, the Busy Body, at your service."

Jack looked at the two of them, feeling very protective for some odd reason. "Maybe you and the little one should crawl into the bottom bunk and get some sleep. I'll use the top one. The rain is starting to slow down, and we can get a little shut eye before the wrecker comes."

He took Brian from her arms, while Sara turned down the blanket. Jack placed the sleepy boy down on the bed and Sara pulled the sheet and blanket over him.

"Thanks, Jack, for everything." Sara gave him a warm smile and slipped in bed beside her sleeping son.

Jack pulled off his boots and crawled up to the top bunk and instantly fell into the deep slumber of a tired man.

Sara lost in her memories, finally fell to sleep, and lulled by the now gently falling rain.

CHAPTER 3

The gears of a noisy truck pulling up next to his rig dragged Jack out of the depths of slumber. It was probably the wrecker. He opened his eyes to see the sun shining brightly through the window. He wasn't surprised to hear knocking on the truck door. He slid down from the bunk. Running his hand through his hair he took the couple of steps to his seat behind the wheel and rolled down the window.

There stood a state patrolman in a brown uniform that looked freshly starched and ironed so the creases stood out, and another man Jack assumed was the wrecker driver by his grease stained clothes. The guy's hat said 'Ernie's Tow and Garage' on it. Luckily the guy had a big head or the whole name wouldn't have shown.

"You the one who called in last night about the car?" the trooper's voice was gruff but his lips smiled as he talked. Jack couldn't see the officer's eyes hidden behind the mirrored glasses. He liked to see a man's eyes.

"Yes sir. The owner of the vehicle and her little boy are sleeping in the..." Jack was interrupted as Sara stepped to his side, still dressed in his clothes, smothering a yawn. Her eyes still sleepy and her hair disheveled.

The trooper stepped closer to the truck and peered at her over the top of his sunglasses. He had a clipboard in his hand that he glanced down at. Looking up at her he quizzed, "Are you Sara Taylor, owner of that dark blue Buick half in the ditch behind this truck?" Evidently he had done a tracer on the license plates.

Sara nodded and explained what transpired.

Satisfied with her story, the trooper jerked his thumb toward the man standing next to him. "Eddy here works for 'Ernie's' and he'll tow the car to the garage. It's about a mile up the road. You have any objections to that?" The trooper asked looking at them both.

"No sir that will be fine. Can my son and I get a ride too?" Sara asked.

"No need for that Sara." Jack interrupted. "I'll give you a ride up to the truck stop. It's just down the road from the garage. Eddy can have the car dropped off there when it's fixed. There is truck stop with showers where you and Brian can get cleaned up." Jack pointed his hand at her. "I don't think my wrinkled shirt is really the fashion rage around here."

Sara looked down and started to blush. She wondered what the trooper and Eddy thought about that.

The trooper cleared his throat, "That plan sounds fine to me."

Sara got her car key out of her jeans and handed it to Jack and told him which suitcases she needed. He got those out of the trunk and handed the car key to Eddy. Then he stowed away his road markers in his truck. In no time, Eddy had the car ready to be towed. It was time to get a move on.

The trooper led the small parade, with Jack next, and Eddy bringing up the rear towing the disabled Buick. As they reached the intersection where the garage was located, the trooper waved good-bye and turned in the opposite direction. His job was done.

Jack pointed out the garage to Sara and continued down the road to the truck stop. Just in time. Brian had to go potty. Now. Real bad.

Sara had changed back into her dry but wrinkled clothes and felt like a mess. Jack stopped the rig and Sara hurried her son into the restroom.

Jack parked the truck and carried their suitcases and his small bag into the building.

After Brian finished, and Sara walked toward the waiting Jack, she never heard all the noise of the truck stop. She just saw a wonderful man who helped her in a time of need. He needed a shave, but he had a nice smile for a man who had little sleep and was no doubt behind schedule because of them. She was feeling guilty about that.

Handing Sara their suitcases, Jack suggested she and Brian have a shower and he would do the same and meet back in the diner area for breakfast. Sara agreed. This was something new. Sara had never showered at a truck stop before.

When Sara and Brian were finished showering and dressed, they walked into the dining area and saw Jack already seated at a table. He was talking on the phone and writing on a pad. Sara hoped he wasn't in trouble with his boss over helping them. He looked up and saw her and motioned them to the table. He hung up the phone just as she was sliding Brian into the booth.

"Hi, let's order breakfast and then I have some things to tell you," Jack remarked as he waved to get the attention of a waitress. They placed their orders and Jack leaned back, notepad in hand.

"I just finished talking to a friend who works and lives in Woodland. She said you were more than welcome to stay with her a few days while you look around the area. She will help you find a job too. Her name is Rosie and she's part-owner of a truck stop there. Nice woman. I have her number here. You can give her a call. I also talked to the garage and they said your alternator is shot. I gave them the go ahead and put in a new one. It will cost this much to replace it," he leaned forward and slid the sheet of paper across the table to her.

"If you don't have the money for the bill, I'll advance it to you." Now why did he say that? First of all, he really didn't know her and here he was offering her some hard earned money he would probably never see again. He must have a screw loose from lack of sleep.

He raised his head at the sound of her laughter. She pointed a finger at him and opened her mouth to say something when another peal of laughter rang out of her. Jack didn't have a clue to what she thought was so funny.

"You! You," Sara gasp between laughs, "You think I'm destitute." She finally got control of herself, wiped her eyes, and reached for his hand with both of hers. "Jack, you are truly a wonderful, caring person. I'm sorry to laugh like this. But Brian and I are okay. Really. I can afford to fix the car and find a place to stay, although it would be nice to meet this friend of yours."

"What I didn't tell you last night, during our therapy session Doctor, that between the liability insurance from the company that Jim worked for, and the fact that Brian and I were left everything in my in-law's will, we are okay financially. But, I thank you so very, very much from the bottom of my heart for your concern and help." She patted his hand. "There aren't many people in the world like you that would go out of their way for total strangers. You're one in a million."

Jack was relieved when Sara was interrupted by the arrival of their breakfast. He was embarrassed and didn't know how to respond to her compliments.

They were finishing their meals when Eddy put in an appearance to tell them the car was outside and ready to go. Eddy stood looking over Sara's shoulder as she signed some travelers checks.

"I looked over the rest of the car, Ma'am, and everything looks fine. Real fine. You might want to get an oil change before too long." Eddy remarked as he handed her the car keys. "I parked the car right across the driveway." He gestured toward the door with his greasy thumb.

"Thank you, Eddy. I appreciate that." Sara smiled at him. "And here's a little extra for bringing my vehicle to me." Sara placed a ten dollar bill on top of the checks.

"No problem Ma'am and thank you for the tip." And with that, Eddy folded the check and stuck it in his shirt pocket, as he sauntered over to the counter. It was coffee and donut time.

Jack eased out of the booth and slowly stood up. "I talked to my next stop and they're waiting for me. I'll take care of the meal and then I have to make some tracks. Here's my cell phone number. Give me a call sometime and let me know how you and the little fella are doing." He ruffled the little boy's hair. Brian suddenly turned shy and ducked behind his mom and peeked back at Jack.

"No way, Jack! Breakfast is on me. After all you have done for us! I won't hear of it." Sara quickly snatched the bill from Jack's hand. "Matter of fact, I owe you some snacks too. If I remember correctly, we cleaned out your little stash of goodies last night."

Jack felt very odd. He had never let a lady buy his meal. But one look at her face told him she was very adamant about it. He nodded okay, knowing she didn't want to feel beholden. He sure hoped no one he knew was at the checkout and saw Sara paying for his food, especially the state trooper.

Sara insisted on picking up some snacks and bottled water for Jack as she choose some for Brian and herself. She loaded up Jack's arms and they carried them to the cashier.

They walked out together. Jack checked out the car, and satisfied, he gave the thumbs up. Sara buckled Brian in his car seat and shut the door.

"Well, I guess it's time we both hit the trail." Jack needed to get on the road and he felt relieved knowing that Sara and her boy would be fine.

Sara stepped up close to Jack and on tip toes; she put her arms around his neck and gave him a big hug. He hugged her back. She smelled good.

"Thanks for everything Jack. You truly are a 'Warrior of the Road'."

"Bye Sara, take good care of yourself and Brian." Jack leaned down and waved at the patient little boy and then he gave a short salute to Sara and headed for his truck. He needed to fuel up and make up some lost time. He turned back and watched as she drove off. *'Warrior of the Road' huh? That sounded nice.* Jack shook his head and smiled inwardly at himself.

'Warrior'. He climbed up into the truck. This big warrior better get this ole horse moving.

CHAPTER 4

Quickly putting his snacks away in the cubby hole, Jack took a few minutes to straighten up his living quarters. This was his home on wheels and he liked it neat and clean. Putting the bundle of clothes that Sara had worn in the dirty clothes bag, Jack could still smell her lingering hint of perfume. Funny how you could miss someone you just met. He tightened the draw string to close the bag, climbed in his seat, and put in a cassette. Time to roll.

Jack knew the way. He had driven this route many times. He would stay on Interstate 5 and then switch to Interstate 40. Barring any road construction delays, Jack wanted to be in Barstow when he shut down for the night. If all went as scheduled, he would be in Santa Fe the following day. You could always make good time going through Arizona.

As Jack drove, he wondered if he would ever hear from Sara again. What had she called him again? Ah yes, 'Warrior of the Road'. He liked her. She was a very attractive, nice young woman. Oh well, he would talk with Rosie on his next trip out and check on Sara and Brian.

The truck was a new one and handled with ease. Jack felt like he and the truck were one. He actually caught himself talking to it. Maybe he should give it a name. Um, Sara had called him a Warrior; maybe he should call it Blackie, his big black shiny steed. He grinned at himself. He needed to talk with people more. A fellow could get in trouble talking to his self all the time. He turned down the volume of the song and clicked on the CB. There was always conversation going on there.

Constantly checking his mirrors and scanning the road ahead was second nature with Jack. He was a defensive driver, always on the watch for the idiot who took dangerous chances. The one who thought his 2,000 pound vehicle was bigger than a trucker's rig. If Jack had a nickel for every driver that would speed up and then cut in front of him, he'd be rich and could retire. When he'd first started to drive, he got upset with them. Now, he just backed off and gave the idiots some space. John Q. Driver needs to learn a truck can't stop on a dime. Jack sighed.

As if on cue, Jack observed in his side mirror, a bright red SUV weaving in and out of the traffic. At first, Jack wasn't sure if the guy was drunk or just plain stupid. He was passing in the no passing zones, staying right on the bumper of the car in front of him until he darted back out into the left lane.

Jack watched the SUV for awhile and finally had enough of the dangerous antics when the SUV recklessly changed lanes again causing the car behind him to hit his breaks which veered the vehicle to the side of the road. At the speed being traveled, Jack marveled the car didn't flip over. Enough was enough and Jack got on the CB. "Hey Reefer Man and White Truck, got your ears on?"

"Affirmative Blackie" came both replies.

"I have a red SUV on my back door that needs to be taught a few road manners. The crazy way he's driving, he is going to cause an accident or be one. How about we box him in for an exit or two and teach him some manners. We'll make him drive the speed limit and stay in one lane." Jack had done this action before with other truckers. So far, no one ever reported them to the state troopers.

"This is White Truck. I'll let those few cars in front of you go by, and then I'll get into the left lane. Reefer Man can hold steady beside me until Mr. Red SUV gets in the left lane. Reefer

Man will drop beside him in the right lane and Blackie, you get behind SUV in the left lane."

That is exactly what the truckers did. If the SUV driver's hand signals meant anything, this was one angry dude. The little convoy of truckers kept him boxed in for two exits before they all agreed maybe he had learned his lesson. At least the naughty hand gestures had stopped. Mr. Red SUV finally figured out he wasn't going anywhere until the truckers let him.

Chuckling, Jack spoke into the CB. "You think Mr. SUV finally learned some road manners?"

"Ten Four Blackie," was the reply, and the truckers pulled back, leaving a doorway for Mr. SUV to take the exit, which he did without any hesitation. All the truckers agreed, sometimes a man has to do what a man has to do. And they did.

Once Jack passed through Bakersfield, CA, he knew it was time to find a place to shut down for the night. He was getting pretty close to Barstow. He had made great time and he was going to treat himself to some tasty food and music. He thought a steak and salad followed by some blues music was a winning idea. He knew of a great place there where they did a lot of jamming. Jack always carried his guitar with him.

Jack pulled into a preferred spot, away from the reefer trucks. These are noisy trucks, but they keep frozen items froze, and cool items from spoiling. Taking time to make sure his log books were up to date, he grabbed his shaving kit and some clean clothes, and headed for a shower and a shave. Man that shaving got to be a pain. He wondered what he would look like in a beard. He rubbed his chin thoughtfully.

After cleaning up, he stowed his things back in the truck and picked up his guitar. He had driven many miles to pay for this beauty. It had quality and a wonderful sound. He had spent untold hours mastering it. He patted his pocket to check for his wallet and keys, locked up, and started walking the couple of blocks to the steak house.

It was an older part of town; a lot of the surrounding buildings were run down. Jack wasn't afraid to be walking alone, it wasn't that bad and he didn't see any groups of shady looking characters hanging around the corners or cruising the streets. He wasn't looking for any fights, nor did he want to lose his guitar. Yet, he'd fight anyone who tried to take it away.

As he approached the restaurant, he could see the parking lot was half full. Well, it was about eight and a week night. In a way that was nice, there shouldn't be too many wanting to join in the jamming.

The restaurant was well kept up for this part of town. The exterior was brick, and the wood trim around the windows and door was painted green. Somehow it radiated character and charm. Jack stepped inside and paused to look around, soaking up the atmosphere. The lighting was subdued. The interior was clean, and thankfully not the glass and Formica like most of the new buildings. Small round wooden tables surrounded the little dance floor and platform where the musicians played. He didn't recognize any of the players. The earthy blues music was the sound for the night. Jack liked the feeling and sound. It had soul.

The waitress was busy, so Jack found a table close to the players and set his guitar case next to the chair. He glanced around the room, taking in the old oak wood trim around the walls, the ancient light fixtures, and photographs of music greats as far back as the 30's. He started to relax as the music seeped into his being. He nodded to the musicians. They smiled back, acknowledging that they had seen his guitar case.

Jack recognized Betty the waitress zigzagging between tables. She held the menu out to him. "Wanna take a look, or have the usual; rib-eye medium well, baked potato, and tossed salad with oil/vinegar dressing on the side?" She smiled knowingly. Betty had been working here for fifteen years. She had a fantastic memory, plus most drivers ordered steak nearly all the time.

"Add an ice tea with lemon to that and we've got a deal." Jack grinned back. Betty left to turn in the order. Jack leaned back and let the music work its magic, releasing the stress of the attempted robbery, Rosie being shot and the mud slide.

It didn't take long and Jack had his meal in front of him. While he was eating, he noticed a few more men about his age come in carrying instruments. They joined a slim woman in her middle twenties at a table right next to the platform. She had short red hair and was wearing a floor length red skirt with a black long sleeved top. No jewelry, simple but elegant. She too was absorbing the music.

Jack finished eating and pushed his plate to one side when he noticed the red head step up to the microphone, and with a sultry voice, began singing. She swayed gently with the rhythm of the song. Jack sat there, mesmerized by her voice. When the song ended, she smiled at those who applauded, nodded, and gracefully stepped down to her table.

Opening the case, Jack picked up his guitar and strummed a chord. Making a slight adjustment, he strummed again. Without making a sound, he ran his fingers through a series of chords to loosen up the fingers. Then he went up and joined the players. As he played, he noticed more people coming in. Some went up to the bar; others took their drinks to the tables.

More and more couples got up to dance. It didn't take long and the small dance floor was crowded. Who could sit with that music flooding over you? You just had to move. The young men at the table with the red head picked up their instruments and joined in. The soulful sound of the sax, trumpet and trombone blended in.

After a few sets, they took a break and Jack looked at his watch, astonished time had passed so quickly. It seemed like he had just started playing. He said goodbye to the other players and placed his guitar in the case. As he straightened up, he saw the redhead standing in front of him. He hadn't heard her approach. Up close she was a knockout.

She extended her hand to shake his, "Enjoyed your music. I haven't seen you around here before." Her voice was gentle, yet moving, like her singing.

Jack shook her hand. "Thanks, I'm a semi driver and don't get around here very often. I like to stop when I can. You have a beautiful voice. Live around here?"

"Thanks, just visiting. My brother is the drummer." She nodded her head at the lanky young man snuggling up to a young blond girl standing at the bar. "Our parents are having their fiftieth wedding anniversary this weekend, so we all came home early to help prepare. I work for a cruise ship, so I can get away pretty easy. We set up our jobs by the week, not the season. It gives us some freedom to do other things."

While they were talking, other musicians started playing again.

Jack glanced at his watch. "It was nice meeting you, but I need to get some shuteye. It's been a long day and I'm getting up early in order to miss the morning traffic rush. There's a company in Santa Fe waiting for my load." He bent to pick up the black case.

Feeling her hand on his arm, Jack paused.

"How about one dance and then you can leave." Her blue eyes smiled at him and she held out her hand. Clearly the answer 'no' to her wasn't an option.

Jack set the case back down, only a crazy man would refuse that offer, and he wasn't *that* crazy, yet. He took her hand and they walked out onto the dance floor. Taking her in his arms, they let the sensual beat of the music direct their steps. They danced well together and made a nice looking couple. The song ended; reluctantly he released her and they sauntered slowly back to the table.

Jack once more picked up his guitar.

"Thanks for the dance, Guitar Man. You dance as well as you play. Maybe we will meet again some time." The redhead smiled.

Jack laughed, "My semi doesn't float very well, but I do take vacations."

She nodded and watched Jack leave the building.

He was half way to his truck when he stopped, turned around, and slapped his forehead. He didn't even know her name. Man, he must be *crazy* after all or getting senile!

CHAPTER 5

Taking a swig of water, Jack began entertaining thoughts about stopping for something to eat. He had been munching on fruit and popcorn all day. After his big breakfast at the truck stop, he didn't want any lunch and besides, it always took so much time to stop. He had pushed hard to get his load to Amarillo, Texas on time. There he picked up a new trailer and would drop it off in Oklahoma City. But for now, he was getting hungry.

Not far from here was a little town of Groom, with a whopping population of five hundred and eighty seven. It is also home to the largest cross in the western hemisphere. At the foot of the cross were life-size bronze Stations of the Cross. West of the Cross was a crucifixion scene up on a hill. East of the cross was a memorial. South of it was a climate controlled building with information regarding the Shroud of Turin. The Cross was sponsored by the Knights of Columbus. The Cross stood 190 feet tall. It was impossible to miss.

If that wasn't awesome enough, located in the same small town was the Leaning Water Tower. It had "Britten, USA" printed on the tower. There is a star and light on the top and a light at the base. History says it was brought to Groom by Ralph Britten to serve as a tourist attraction and a reason for people to stop at his truck stop. The truck stop was gone, but the water tower remained.

But to Jack, in Groom, the best homemade burritos he had ever tasted in his life could be found. His mouth watered just thinking about it. He would spend the night here.

Turning on the radio for a country-wide weather report, he heard that tomorrow should be a good driving day, although the middle states were getting some light snow. Jack hoped it would quit snowing by the time he got there. The longer he could get by without putting on chains the better.

Shifting down, Jack pulled off the Interstate 40. 'Casa de Maria' was his destination. His growling stomach told him he would eat now, take a walk and be back to the semi for an early bedtime.

One of Maria's sons was a trucker too, and that's how Jack had heard about the small cafe. He gave it a try once. Now he always stopped when he could and recommended it to other drivers. He was their unpaid advertiser for the marvelous Mexican food.

Parking down the street so that his big rig wouldn't take up most of her parking area, Jack stiffly climbed down out of the cab, stretched and twisted. Then he locked the truck. It felt good to be out of the truck and walk.

The little cow bell tinkled 'welcome' as Jack opened the door and stepped into the unique cafe. Maria had it completely decorated in Mexican motif. Actually, she used familiar things; it was her home away from home. She wanted the patrons to feel as though they were guests in her casa. That was the warm atmosphere Jack felt too as he walked through the door to inhale a mixture of mouth-watering aromas.

"Señor Jack!" Maria came bustling out from the door way that leading from the kitchen. She raised her plump arms up to hug him. Jack leaned down and hugged her back, then tightening his grip, picked her up and swung her around.

"Put me down, Jack! Papa! Señor Jack is here!" Mariá excitedly called out. She was happy to see this young hombre. She caught her breath as Jack gently lowered her feet to the floor.

All smiles, Roberto wearing his usual black slacks, white ruffled shirt, bolo tie and white apron tied around his waist, joined them and pumping Jack's hand vigorously up and down. "Buenas noches, Señor Jack. Welcome! Come, a seat." He pulled out a chair and gestured for Jack to sit.

"Momma, this hombre tiene hambre; some food, some food for our Jack!" Roberto was very excited, Jack wasn't just a customer to them, but like a son.

Mariá smiled, "I get you mucho food." She shook her head, "You too skinny, Señor Jack. I get you a grande meal." She scurried off, her long colorful skirt swirling around her legs.

"I haven't seen José on the road lately. Did he change companies or quit driving?" Jack questioned Roberto who by now had calmed down had taken a seat at the table.

Roberto leaned closer to Jack, "Ah, my poor José. You not hear?" Roberto's eyes got shinny, and he blinked fast a few times before continuing. "Two months ago, José was coming down a steep mountain road. The brakes gave out. He steered into the hill instead of going over the side, but at the speed the truck was going when it hit the rock, he ended up with some broken ribs, and one fractured leg. He will not be driving for awhile. We could have lost him." Roberto made the sign of the cross. "We say many prayers to San Roquè. His momma and I don't want him back on the road." Roberto stopped then, realizing he was talking to a man who took these same risks every day.

Jack knew what Roberto was thinking and squeezed the old gentleman's arm.

"Will José will be okay? Does he just need to have some physical therapy?" Concern filled Jack's voice. "Has he lost the desire to drive?"

Shaking his head no, Roberto smiled. "José say, 'Papa, trucking is in my blood. How could I ever stay in one place? Every day, I would drive to a building, work all day shut out from the sun, then drive back home. If I could not drive my semi I would not breathe, or vivir. No, Papa, I need the freedom and challenge of the road'." Roberto shrugged his shoulders.

Maria entered through the archway carrying a huge tray laded with many filled dishes and set them on the table. Roberto helped her arrange them. True to her word, she was going to fatten Jack up.

Jack took a huge sniff as he looked over the food. "Ah Maria, a meal fit for a King."

Maria and Roberto stood side by side, beaming with wide-eyed pride.

"Eat, eat, Señor; there is more where that came from." Maria nervously wiped her hands on her apron as Jack took his first bite. She loved to watch his reaction to her food. She wasn't disappointed as Jack brought his fingers to his lips, kissed them and pointed to Maria.

"Maria, if you weren't already married to Roberto, I would carry you away."

"Oh, Señor Jack." Maria was at once embarrassed, honored and pleased.

Roberto proudly put his arm around the shoulders of his wife and gave her a squeeze. "Señor Jack, you need to find a señorita like my Maria."

Jack laughed, "Sí Roberto, but there aren't any more left like Maria."

They were interrupted by the door bell and in came José using a pair of crutches, followed closely by a beautiful young lady with long thick black hair that flowed down to her waist.

"José!" Jack stood up so quickly the chair nearly tipped over. He walked over and shook José's hand and gave him a manly hug. "Glad to see you amigo! Come join me while I eat this magn'fica food your mama has prepared." He gestured at the table. "And tell me all about that." He pointed at the leg in the cast.

"Mama called and said you were here. Thought I'd hobble over and see how the trucking world is doing without me." José laughed handing his crutches to the young lady, and carefully sat down. She immediately pulled out a chair for him to put his leg up on. He smiled at her with eyes full of love. "Angelica spoils me."

Jack sat back down. Maria had brought out some more plates, and they all shared the tasty meal as José told Jack about the accident.

"It was loco how it happened. You know how careful I am about checking out my rig, especially pulling through the mountains. The only theory the investigators could come up with is there must have been a small pin hole leak in the brake line. Even though I had shifted down to low gear, the amount of pressure on the brake pedal was all it took. I tell you for un momento, I was pretty busy, driving and praying. I wasn't sure if there was going to be a mañana for me. I guess my prayers were answered that no car or truck was coming up the mountain; we all would have gone over the edge since I was taking the whole road. There really wasn't any choice. Either hit the side of the mountain before I gained any more speed, or go over the side. No matter how hard I prayed, I didn't think wings were going to sprout on the truck."

"When I came to, they had me on the stretcher. Now I know how the matador feels when the angry bull uses him to play ball." José smiled. "My ribs are healing and," he patted his cast, "This comes off mañana and the physical therapy starts. I came out much better than the truck. The cab was totaled, but the trailer and contents were okay. Would you believe I was transporting a load of mattresses? My boss said I can come back when the doc signs my release, and I can pass the CDL physical."

José saw his mama and papa exchange frightened looks and stopped talking.

Angelica was shaking her head, her long black hair gently swaying. She didn't want her José back on the road. She was afraid that next time there was an accident, he might die. You could tell the way the love shone from her eyes when she looked at Jose' that she was very much in love with him.

Feeling caught between the two different opinions, Jack looked at both of them. As a driver, he knew how José felt, yet, he could understand how Angelica and José's parents worried. Jack cleared his throat, "Sometimes you have to let a man be a man. José will know when it is time to come off the road for good, maybe when the bebe' come."

Angelica started to blush and shyly lowered her head, her eyes glancing over at José.

José smiled, and Roberto and Maria sighed and nodded. A little bebé would be nice.

Jack glanced at his watch, the time had flown by. "My amigos, I must leave your pleasant company. I have a lot of miles to cover tomorrow. Where's my bill Roberto?"

Roberto shook his head no. He reached behind a door and brought out an old scarred up guitar. "One song, Señor Jack is the price of the meal. Momma and I have missed your beautiful playing."

Jack paid his bill in full, plus a nice tip.

CHAPTER 6

Pulling back on to Interstate 40, Jack's next stop would be Oklahoma City. Scanning his side mirrors for any unusual traffic, Jack smiled to himself, "I'm making good time. Once I drop this trailer off and pick up the next one, I'll have a straight shot back to Wisconsin and a few days of needed rest."

His pleasant idea of time off disappeared as the bane of the trucker had its open light on. The Department of Transportation was in business. Jack groaned as he geared down and pulled into line. "Why now? Everything was going smoothly. Oh geez! Five semis in front of me, I wonder how much time this will take?"

He knew his log was up to date and the truck was new and performing fine. Everything was in order back in Santa Fe, having weighed his truck before he left that stop, and all the required paper work was in the briefcase. It was just a time-consuming hassle, but he realized it was a necessary evil. Some truckers or companies wouldn't keep up the equipment if the D.O.T. wasn't there forcing them to comply. There were huge fines for the drivers or companies that weren't in compliance. Who wants unsafe drivers or vehicles on the road? Not Jack. He had witnessed the results of poorly maintained trucks and overtired or medicated drivers. It was never a pretty sight.

He let out a long sigh. "As long as I have to wait, I might as well check and see how long the receiving dock is open at the Treboe Company."

A female voice answered the phone. "Good afternoon, Treboe Company. How may I help you?"

"Hi, I'm Jack O'Ryan, with a load due for your company today. The D.O.T has their light on and I'm the fifth truck in line. Would I still be able to unload later this evening?"

"Hold please," a feminine voice replied.

Within seconds, the warehouse manager came on the line. "Don, speaking. Say, I really would appreciate it if you could get that load here tonight. We need it for production first thing in the morning."

"If all goes well, I should get there about nine tonight. Will that be okay?" Jack responded.

"Great, that will work out fine. Thank you. I will notify the night shift to unload you the minute you arrive, and I will also alert the security guard to let you in. Tell him I want you at dock five." He then gave Jack his direct number to call if there was a problem of any kind.

While Jack waited for his turn to have the semi checked, he ate some lunch he had heated up in his little food warmer. The neat little heater resembled an old lunch bucket that plugged into the cigarette lighter outlet.

Then he pulled out his guitar and did some strumming. He had a song he was working on. It was better than being frustrated at the delay.

Jack had his window down and pretty soon a couple of drivers came up to the truck thinking he had some good music on tape, only to find it was live.

"Hey, man, sounding good. How long you been pickin'? Know any country western songs?" The man wore scuffed up cowboy boots and an old brown wide brim hat with a snake skin band on it. "I like country, I grew up on it," he said with a friendly smile.

They talked awhile. Truckers are a special group of people and they swapped stories of living and driving on the road.

"Sure hope they don't take all day with the inspections. Last week I had some young upstart go through my rig with a fine tooth comb. Just because they put on a uniform and get paid by the state, they think they can do anything they want too. The darn kid even pulled the sheets off the bed and dumped out my dirty clothes bag. Sure didn't appreciate my dirty underwear underfoot. Since my log and papers were up to date, there wasn't any reason for it! Do I look like I'm the type to have dope or weapons in my rig?" The older gentleman looked similar to Kenny Rogers, the singer, not some smuggler or dope peddler.

Greg, the country western music lover spoke up, "I hear yah man. Any of you get pulled over by a portable scale set up?"

Coffee Man, (the CB handle the driver went by) leaning against the door, replied, "You bet! Had a costly experience a month back. I was driving through this little ole state that evidently wanted some of my hard earned money. They had the sign out and I stopped. Of course they said I was overloaded. I knew I wasn't because I weighed the truck before I left the last stop."

The men were all nodding their heads in unison.

"Those portable units should be outlawed because they aren't accurate anyway. You can drive the same truck over the scales three times in succession, and get three different weights, because the scales are set up on the side of the road where it isn't level. Therefore, it's not a legal weight scale. To add insult to misery, these aren't D.O.T. men, but a hired out team with no real government authority." Coffee Man's voice was tinged with anger.

He continued, "It ticked me off royally, gave me a real big pain in the backside. They know they have you over a barrel. Pay the fine, or lose a couple days of work, plus lawyer fees. I called my company and they decided it was time to fight it. We have too many trucks delivering through there to be messed with."

"So what happened?" Jack asked.

"We went to court and the judge threw the case out and my company ain't been bothered since." Coffee Man smiled. "Of course, the lawyer didn't work for the fun of it."

The next truck pulled ahead and the men went back to their own rigs.

Only one truck was pulled over to the side and got a thorough check from front to back. The rest of them just had the weight and their logs checked. Jack was on the road again.

He set the cruise, put in the CD by ***Jim Brickman***, called 'Simple Things', singing along as the miles rolled by.

Jack wondered how Rosie was doing and mused over the young lady, Sara, and her son, Brian. Oh yes, and that pretty redhead that sang the blues. She sure had a beautiful voice. He shook his head remembering he didn't get her name and number. He chuckled to himself, "Maybe this was a sign of old age."

The traffic was thinning out. The weather was fine. If it continued like this, he would make it back to Wisconsin in time for Thanksgiving after all. His sister was having all the family over to her house this year.

Night had fallen by the time he reached the suburbs outside of Oklahoma City. He noticed directions to the company weren't written on the invoice, and he forgot to ask when he had called about the delivery time. "Man, I must be getting old, twice in one week I forget to ask a question. First the name of redhead singer, and now for directions," Jack mused as he got on the CB and asked about the location.

Someone came on with the handle of Big Buster.

"I just delivered a load a few blocks from there. You keep going until you come to the third stop-light. Take a right and go about a mile. You can't miss it. They have the company name up in so many lights you'd think it was Christmas."

"Thanks Big Buster. Ten-four."

Jack had no problem finding the place. The large brightly lit sign was above the security gate. "I'd hate to have to pay their electricity bill," Jack said aloud as he brought the big black rig up to the gate stopped and rolled down the window.

The elderly guard leaned out of the security shack, and peered at the logo on the truck. "Evenin' young fellow. What dock are you looking to unload at?"

"Dock five, sir."

The old gentleman gave a low chuckle, "Guess you're the one they're waiting for. Just go ahead son. I'll call and let them know you're on the way." He slowly pulled his upper torso back out of the window and pushed the button for the gate to open, and with his thin arm, waved Jack through.

Shaking his head, Jack wondered how old the security guard was. Physically he wouldn't be able to protect himself from a net full of butterflies if he had too much less someone trying to crash the gate. Fortunately, all the old man had to do was push buttons and stay awake. Jack smiled to himself and bet the man had a small television in there someplace and a thermos of hot chocolate. He had to give him credit for working at his age.

Jack found the dock with no problem, and expertly backed the semi in dock five. It was a tight squeeze with a rig on either side of him.

An overweight worker slowly ambled out of a side door and leaned back against the wall. "You want to unload tonight so you can get going?" He had a smirk on his face and talked with a toothpick between his lips. By the look of his protruding abdomen, it had been a long time since he had unloaded anything but a candy bar from its wrapper.

Jack shook his head in annoyance. He had dealt with this type many times before: lazy, dishonest, and a bully. Tonight, this slob irritated Jack. He was tired and really didn't feel like dealing with a loser trying to cheat him out of money.

Jack spun around from unlocking the trailer doors and stepped right up to the heavy man. His normally good disposition had disappeared. "No, I want to get unloaded TONIGHT because YOU need the product I have on my truck." Jack said this very slowly through clenched jaws. He knew this sleaze ball was going to try and hit him up for lumper pay. Pay extra or sit and wait. In a trucker's life, when the wheels aren't rolling, you don't make any money. But Jack wasn't going to pay him extra to do his job. The man was getting paid to unload and Jack could sit all night. He was out of hours anyway. No skin off his nose either way. But sleaze ball didn't know this. The man DID KNOW that the load held materials needed in the plant and was just trying to pull a scam.

Pulling away from the wall, sleeze ball inspected his dirty nails, and in a very insincere tone he replied, "Well, we're kinda busy right now, but for fifty bucks, I could unload..." The man's voice trailed off.

Jack stepped right up into the man's face, all six foot two inches of him. "I'm tired, I want a shower, and I'm not going to put up with a scumbag like you. You can unload me NOW, sign this bill of lading and I'm out of here, or you can call 911 because you can't work very well with a broken arm."

Jack watched the fat man's face blanch as he stumbled back a step. His scam to cheat money out of drivers wasn't working with this young man.

Two other employees were peering around the side door. The jerk cleared his throat, "Harry, Jim, quit loafing, get the fork-lift, and unload this truck, pronto." He scribbled his name on the sheet, took a copy of the bill, and for a heavy man, disappeared quickly into the building.

Jack didn't see hide nor hair of him again.

The man that Jack assumed was Harry stepped lively over to Jack. Jerking his thumb in the direction of the vanishing night dock supervisor, cleared his throat, then rechecked to make sure no one could hear him. He stuttered, "Ed, Ed, there gets mi- mi- mighty testy if we st- st- start to unload before he says so. Me, me, and Jim will have your trailer unloaded ri- ri- right away. Yep, right away."

Jack nodded to the man as Jim positioned the fork-lift to start unloading. He understood how working conditions were in some places. Maybe a little birdie ought to let the office manager know what was going on. He would think about that. He did have that direct number.

Fifteen minutes later, the truck was empty and Jack was ready to pull out. Harry gave him directions where to drop this empty trailer and pick up the full one. Jack felt bad for losing his temper, but he didn't like to be taken advantage of either.

Stopping at the gate, Jack waved to the old man. Making a right turn, Jack headed for a truck stop, hoping there would still be a space there for him. He needed some sleep.

Jack found a place and wearily pulled into it. The weather was nice. He thought he would shut the rig down, and leave a vent open to let the cool fresh night air permeate the cab.

As he was getting ready for bed, he heard some loud angry voices. Jack paused and listened, to assure himself no one was messing with his truck or load.

Disturbing the quite night was a woman's shrill high voice yelling, "Don't tell me you weren't flirting with that cheap little hussy. Yah think I'm blind and deaf? I wasn't born yesterday you know."

"Pipe down. You're imagining things again. Go to sleep. I need to get some sleep." The male voice responded.

"Sure, you want to go to sleep and dream of that short-skirted waitress with the big boobs. I know you like a book Honey." Her voice was harsh and louder.

"Shut up, Louise. From now on you can pay for all the meals. You can even wear my pants and be the man of the family. Will that make you happy? Now, for the last time, shut up and go to sleep."

Jack knew he had parked next to a married couple that team drove. Oh great. Those two were known for their arguing. Should he pull out and find an empty lot somewhere, knock on their door and risk getting drawn into their fight, or just call security?

Jack started his truck up again, hoping the sounds would muffle his neighbor's disagreement. Then he put in a soothing CD that he liked. Pulling off his boots, Jack laid on top of the covers. Hopefully he could get to sleep. If not, then he would call security. At least it didn't sound like anyone was getting knocked around. Then he definitely would have to intervene.

When Jack woke up, the semi with the bickering couple was gone. Jack wondered if they had kissed and made up, or the husband was so tired he just tuned Louise out and went to sleep. There was something to be said about driving solo.

CHAPTER 7

In the morning, after his breakfast, Jack typed in his location. His computer told him that there was a change of plans and he was to drop this load at Kansas City, MO. From there he would be driving an empty trailer to Sioux Falls, SD where he would pick up a loaded reefer truck. *'Man, I hate those refrigerated trucks,'* Jack groaned. *One never knew when something would go wrong with the controls.* He had to check the temperatures all the time and if the unit did break down, it was a given that it would be at night or on the weekend, when it was almost impossible to find someone to come out right away to fix it. It didn't take long before you had a full load of food that wasn't any good and had to be dumped. The businesses and insurance companies didn't appreciate that one iota.

The weather forecast for wind and snow added to his negative thoughts. Loads of it was predicted. Bummer. What a time to be driving across that flat land with an empty trailer. More times during the years than he cared to think about, he'd had to pull off because the D.O.T. shut down the interstates due to dangerous conditions. He checked to make sure the chains were okay in case he needed them, got his winter boots and warmer coat ready, said his prayer, and took off. Gotta have God as your co-pilot, the only way to drive.

Nine long weary hours later, Jack pulled into a truck stop in Omaha, NE with the empty trailer covered in snow. The weatherman had been right on the money, and he had driven into the wind and snow. His eyes hurt from the strain of trying to see the road with the thick, heavy snowflakes bombarding the window, and the hypnotic rhythm of the wipers as they went back and forth trying to keep the window free. Jack kept his speed down so the wind didn't whip his trailer out of his control, and he constantly watched for other drivers going too fast for the slippery conditions. The last thing he needed was to have the trailer jackknife into the other lane and hit a vehicle or flip him over.

The temperature had steadily dropped during the day. Jack would fuel up before parking for the night. He didn't want his truck freezing up. He pulled into the fuel line. Before he got out of the cab, he put a clean pair of jeans, sweatshirt, some long johns and socks in his overnight bag. Jack wanted his bag ready when he was through fueling the truck. He put on his winter coat, hat, and stepped out into blustery weather.

Jack shivered, the freezing wind whipping over him as he poured fuel additive into the tank to keep the diesel from jelling and freezing up. Having inserted the gas credit card, Jack proceeded to fill both fuel tanks. His fingers were getting numb by the time he finished, even though he had fleece-lined gloves on. He was glad he had put on the ski mask so only his eyes were exposed. By the time Jack was finished he looked like a snowman. He wiped the snow from the door and climbed into the cab. What a relief it was to be out of that unrelenting wind. He pulled off his gloves and rubbed his hands to get some feeling back. The warm air felt good.

Pulling out of the fuel lanes, Jack parked, keeping the cab out of the fierce blowing wind. Shutting down all the lights except for the parking ones, he left the heat on low and the engine idling. All the truckers left their trucks running when it was this cold. Pulling on his warm gloves, he picked up his bag, and reluctantly stepped out once more into the frigid air. Locking the truck, he looked around and headed briskly towards the well lit building.

A hot shower helped to relax and warm him. His stomach rumbled, which reminded him it was time to amble down and order dinner. Maybe he would climb back up the stairs and see a movie before he settled in the truck for the night. With the storm raging like it was outside, no one would be driving tonight.

He paused at the entry way and scanned the place for any familiar faces. "Jack! Jack, over here."

Jack found the face that went with that low gravelly smokers voice. Smiling, he saundered over to the only female trucker he thought could drive like a man, Lou.

He had known her for about six years. She stood about five feet six inches. Her long brown hair was kept in a single braid that usually hung down her back or worn coiled under a western hat. Her uniform was usually jeans and a long sleeve shirt with a vest of some kind, and earrings. Her one concession to femininity was her turquoise earrings. She was the only independent female trucker he would ever trust to drive his rig. Lou was one tough old cookie. She didn't take squat from anyone. Lou could be thirty-five or fifty-five, Jack didn't know and he sure wasn't going to ask her, he liked living.

"How yah doing, Honey, ain't seen you in a coon's age. You made your fortune and only drive in snowy weather now." Lou laughed and gave him a friendly punch on the arm.

"Hey, that's my shifting arm, Woman." Jack feigned a sore arm and sat down across from Lou. "I'm doin' fine, Lou, how about yourself?"

Lou leaned back against the booth and squinting her eyes as she took a deep drag on her cigarette, and slowly expelled the smoke before she spoke. "Can't complain."

Jack shook his head, and fanned the air with his hand, then pointed at the cigarette. "You're gonna kill yourself woman and the rest of us with you if you keep puffing on those things."

"Jack Honey, I gotta go sometime and somehow. Just be glad I don't chew. Then I would have to carry a spittin' cup around."

Jack groaned. The picture of that in his mind was enough to take away his appetite.

Lou continued, "Now, you just hush your trap and sit upwind of the smoke. I was just about to place my order. They have roast beef, mashed taters and gravy as their special. And I love their banana cream pie. It's almost as good as my own."

Putting on a mock surprised look, Jack exclaimed, "Almost as good as your own? You can cook? A pie?" Jack shook his head. "Well, well, will wonders never cease? And here I thought changing oil was your game."

Lou leaned back and let out her husky laugh. "You'd be surprised at all the hidden talents I have, young man."

Just then the waitress approached their table. She pulled out the pencil that had been jammed into her hairdo and poised it above her order pad. Her face relayed a sense of boredom, or maybe she was just tired. Jack wasn't sure.

"Roast beef dinner is the special tonight, or do you want to see a menu?" Her voice was monotone. She didn't even look at him.

A blind man could tell she wasn't going to get many tips with that attitude. Before Jack could reply, Lou spoke up.

"Me and the boy here," Lou nodded her head at Jack, "Will take the roast beef dinner, extra gravy on the potatoes and meat, forget those mushy cooked vegetables and bring the coleslaw and some real cow's cream for the coffee, not that artificial stuff. Bring us a pot of coffee, those little cups don't hold more than a swallow; and if it won't crack your face, Missy, you could give us a smile unless your feet hurt or your dog died." Lou didn't mince words.

"Right away." The waitress rammed the pencil back into her hair, spun around and walked away in a huff.

"I don't remember saying I wanted roast beef and gravy, woman. All that heavy stuff is gonna clog up your arteries. Why I can hear them hardening from here and what do you mean calling me Boy?" Jack waited for her reply. He loved teasing her.

Lou flicked the ashes off the cigarette into the ashtray with a tap of her finger and narrowing her eyes at him as she slowly drew in another drag. "Now, you need something more substantial in this kind of weather than some old salad or sandwich they have around here, and Kid," she paused and coughed, "Anyone more than ten years younger than me, I can call boy or girl. Got it?"

Jack put an exaggerated look of fear on his face, and threw up his hands in mock surrender. "Got it! Does this mean I have to call you Mom?"

"Only if you're going to pay my supper bill, SON," Lou was quick with the comeback.

The unfriendly waitress showed up about that time with their coffee and cream. Placing both hands on the table, she leaned down and looked at Lou. "For your information lady, my boyfriend left me today, right after I told him he was going to be a daddy. No, I don't feel much like smiling. Sorry if I was rude and upset you."

There was a moment of silence, and as the girl turned to leave Lou caught her arm. "Sit down, Gal. Let's talk."

"Let go of my arm Lady. You want to get me fired? You can't do anything for me anyway. Nobody can. I made a bad choice." She shrugged her shoulders. "Anyway, it's my problem. Your food should be ready." She jerked her arm free from Lou's grasp and quickly walked away.

Jack and Lou exchanged looks and Lou shook her head. "Well, what do you think of that? Maybe we should find out who the daddy is and pay him a visit. You know, teach him some manners and about responsibilities," Lou growled out through clinched teeth.

"Personally, I think we ought to keep our nose out of her business. I've grown accustomed to mine being in the middle of my face without any bends and turns and doing what it is suppose to do, like let me breath, not be a target." He leaned back.

"You some kind of pantywaist, a wimp, 'fraid to fight? Maybe you got yourself a contract with some modeling agency." Lou snorted, "Some trucker. Let me see your CDL."

This was a different side of Lou that Jack had never encountered before. He wondered what was behind it. He picked up the coffee carafe and poured a cup, slid it over to her, and then filled his own cup. Lou poured a generous amount of cream in her cup and slowly stirred it. Jack just shook his head. She was going to have a heart attack with the way she ate and smoked.

Jack took a deep breath and broke the silence, "Well, I think that maybe if they would have waited until they took a trip down the church aisle and she had a ring on her finger before they played house, she wouldn't have been in this situation. I have enough going on in my life without taking on somebody else's problems. She was a party to her problem, and she will have to find a solution to it. I'm not her big brother." He took a swig of his coffee and burnt his tongue, probably served him right.

Lou pointed her finger at Jack. "And I think you don't have the foggiest idea in God's green acres of what it is like to be pregnant and left alone. You guys are all the same. Good at planting the seed, then walkin' away and leaving the harvesting for the woman." Lou was visibly upset. She was angry, *real* angry. Jack had never seen her this way.

Throwing caution to the wind, Jack ventured, "Voice of experience Lou?"

"Damned right Kid," Lou snapped at him. "Thirty years ago. Only then, it wasn't accepted like it is now a days. All unwed pregnant girls were naughty girls. The guys had a notch on their belt and they were okay, but the girl was bad." Lou ground out her cigarette like it was the villain.

"Sorry, I shouldn't have said that Lou. I didn't mean to dredge up old memories." *When would he ever learn to think before he spoke. He never meant to hurt her.*

Lou kept on talking, like Jack had never spoken. "I gave him up for adoption. He was a cute little boy. My folks kicked me out when they caught me throwing up one morning and figured I was expecting. The love of my life didn't want to get married either. His plans didn't include a wife and kid. At least I was smart enough to know I couldn't take care of the baby like he needed. The couple, who adopted him, took me in and I lived there until he was born. They gave me some money; I moved to a different town and worked hard. Once a year they send me a picture of him. He is one handsome man, looks a lot like my brother Jared. My boy has a family of his own. He doesn't know about me."

"Anyway, I started working for a trucking firm and found out there was more money to be made driving than riding a desk chair and answering phones. Saved my money and bought my own rig and here I am. And that's why I can identify with this young girl and her dilemma. She is hurt, afraid, and hasn't anyone there for her." Lou paused, "And I don't ever want to hear one word of my story ever leave your lips. Got it?" Lou had a look on her face that demanded the right answer.

"Got it Lou, your story is safe with me." Jack always kept his word. He reached over and patted her hand. "I think you are a very gutsy lady. Not many women are as strong as you are."

Lou nodded at him. She had never told anyone about this before.

The food came then, and they ate in silence, only Jack didn't have much of an appetite anymore. Women. No sense trying to figure them out. They were too full of surprises.

Jack broke down and had a piece of pie with Lou, but he drew the line at any more coffee and asked for some tea which Lou thought was very hilarious.

"Tea, tea? Truckers don't drink tea. That's a ladies' drink." Lou shook her head in amazement. "How you gonna put hair on your chest with that stuff?" She pointed at the tea.

"You been lookin' in the men's showers again Lou? Shame on you." Jack tossed back at her. "Don't knock it unless you try it," he said pushing his mug of tea towards her. "And I want to know how much hair you have on your chest drinking all that rut gut coffee? I don't go peeking in the ladies showers, so I don't know about those things."

Lou sputtered, "Ain't gentlemanly to talk like that to a lady." She shook a cigarette out of the pack and lit it. She took a deep drag and turned her head so the smoke blew away from Jack.

She decided to change the subject. "So, are you headed out now or going to be smart and stay put for the night? Weatherman says it's not fit weather out there for man or beast."

"Naw, I plan to stay put and leave in the morning. I'm out of hours anyway. Besides the road crews should have the roads cleared early. It took me twice as long to get here as it should have. Might as well relax and get a good night sleep when I can. Matter of fact, I was thinking about going upstairs and see what movies were on. Want to join me?"

"Tell you what Kid, you go on up and see if the movie is something my delicate eyes can watch or not. I see our little momma over there is done with her shift and I want to have a talk with her. I'll check in with you after that." Lou was sliding out of the booth.

"Okay, later then." Jack got up too and went upstairs, wondering what Lou had to say to the little momma.

Lou arrived just as the movie ended.

"Lou, you always stand up a man who asks you out to a movie?" Jack slowly stood up and stretched. "You trying to ruin my reputation for being a Lady Killer?" Several of the other truckers who'd also been watching the movie started to snicker.

Lou snorted, "Boy, when you grow out of your knee pants, then we'll talk." The truckers really guffawed at that. Jack's face turned red. He had that one coming.

Grabbing his arm, Lou pulled Jack away from the others and propelled him towards an area that had some privacy.

"Jack, I need to talk with you, I did something and want to run it by you." Lou had a hint of excitement in her voice.

"I think that's a little like shutting the barn door after the horse is out." Jack thought he was clever.

"Shut up, Kid, and listen." Lou reached into her pocket of her shirt for a cigarette. "I thought of a way to help little Momma, the waitress." She shook out one and lit it and took a deep drag on the cigarette. Jack waited for her to cough. She just exhaled the smoke. At least she didn't let it come out of her nose like the guys did.

"Remember I told you about the couple who stood by me when I was pregnant? Well, I gave them a call. It seems like they could use a little help right now. He had a heart attack and had to quit work. He has some physical therapy to do. The Missus is still working and they could use someone to be there, drive him to therapy and all. I suggested that maybe little Momma could move in and help them out, and with all the programs they know about, they could in turn, be with her through the pregnancy and with a new life. Maybe even help with the baby unless she gives it up." Lou's eyes were excited. "So, I talked with little Momma and she thinks it is a good idea too. "What do think of my night's work?"

Stunned, Jack just looked at her. In the space of ninety minutes, Lou had just changed the destiny of three, make that three plus lives, while he watched a movie.

"How on earth did you convince everyone that this is what they wanted or needed in the space of ninety minutes? Woman, you amaze me." Jack continued to look at her.

"I told the little missy to give notice to the boss. She shouldn't be on her legs all the time like that anyway. I'm swingin' back this way next week. I'll have a bit of space in the back of the trailer for her few things. Then I will drop her off at the Anderson's place. Did I tell you they invited me for Thanksgiving?" Lou was just full of surprises.

"This will be rather tough for me, it will be the first time to see my boy in person after all of these years and I can't let him know who I am. The Anderson's will say I am just helping little Momma get there." Lou momentarily got a sad look on her face.

"Lou, you gonna be okay," Jack's voice was full of concern. No matter how gruff and tough Lou tried to act, she was *still* a woman, she *still* had feelings, and she *still* felt alone.

"Yeah, Kid, I'll be okay. I just think this might be a new road in my life. I can sorta be a part-time mom to her and, as a reward get to see my son once in a while. And when the little one comes, hey, I can call myself Grandma. Pretty good for an old broad like me." The tears glistened in her eyes and she quickly wiped them on her sleeve.

Jack put his arms around her and rested his chin on her head. "Yeah, I'd say that was pretty good work, Lady".

CHAPTER 8

Jack woke up to a snow covered world. He stretched and groaned. No sense lying here any longer. Better get up and see how bad it had stormed over night. He opened up the curtain that kept his bunk area dark. The sun was so bright it hurt his eyes. Jack dressed and cleared the snow off the truck, then went in for breakfast.

He looked around for Lou and little Momma but didn't see either one. Lou must have left early. He ate a warm breakfast of oatmeal, toast and a banana. Going back out into the crisp air, he felt like a young colt. He took a deep breath, and was glad to be alive. He got into the truck, said his road prayer, and headed for Sioux Falls.

The roads had been plowed and salted. The right lane had most of the snow worn off already. Traffic was rolling at a pretty good clip. Normally Jack would have been one of the first truckers on the road, but his appointment time wasn't until later, so he figured he might as well sleep in rather than get there too early and have to wait. It was very hard to rest with the noise of all the other trucks and the reefers coming and going, especially, the older models. Those truckers either had to be hard of hearing or somehow had gotten accustomed to it.

Jack made good time and pulled into the lot. He strolled into the office. This was a trucker friendly office. They always had a coffee pot on and some rolls and seasonal fruit sitting out. They even had a phone and computer the drivers could use: a very unusual place. The scenery wasn't bad either and he wasn't referring to the pictures on the walls, as the cutest blond in Sioux Falls stepped up to the counter. If her bright blue sweater was any tighter, Jack was positive it would have been painted on, not that he was complaining. She leaned on the counter as Jack signed in.

"It's been a long time, Jack, since you had a pick up here." Her voice cooed softly. She glanced at him in a coy manner. "Sure hope it wasn't because we didn't have your favorite filled pastry last time you were here."

Jack leaned his elbows on the counter, close to her. "Krissy, with someone as sweet as you here, we don't need any donuts." Um, she smelled good.

Krissy liked the attention. "Well, aren't you the sweet talker?" She gave him a real nice smile as she turned to answer the ringing phone.

Jack watched her as she gave directions over the phone to another trucker. Watching her wasn't hard. The blue sweater and black tight pants gave him plenty to observe. She tossed back her long blond hair, leaned over and made a notation on a sheet of paper.

Krissy hung up the phone and picked up the paper and sauntered back to Jack. "Too bad you have to leave with this load right away. There's a really neat country western concert in town tonight."

"Oh Krissy, now you tell me. Gee, I think I might be coming down with a cold and shouldn't be driving today or tonight. I better stay in town." Jack put his hand to his forehead and faked a cough.

She laughed wishing he would stay too. She had been trying to get a date with him for quite awhile. But, business was business.

"Maybe another time, Krissy. If I'm lucky, I can get this load delivered and make it home in time for Thanksgiving with my family. You know turkey, dressing, and pumpkin pie with whipped cream on it. Now, where do you want me to drop that empty trailer and pick up the loaded one?" Jack smiled at her. He hadn't moved a muscle and neither had she.

She raised her hand and put it on his forehead. "Sure you don't have a fever?" She looked at him shyly through her lashes.

Jack reached up and took her hand, turned her palm up and gave it a kiss. Then he straightened up. "Oh, you can give a guy a fever, girl, and it's really tempting, but I need to get on the road. You know, Mom and the pumpkin pie thing."

Krissy sighed and gave him a pouting look. Nice lips Jack thought. Kissable lips. He wondered if she would give him a sample.

She glanced down at her paper. "Never let it be said that I kept you from making it home for Thanksgiving." She sighed. "Take the empty to lot two and pick up trailer 161 at the dock, door three." She slid the large envelope with all the necessary paper work over to him. "Give me a call next time you are in the area, we always have a lot of concerts, and I really do hope you make it home in time. We couldn't disappoint Mom and not get any pumpkin pie. And Jack, drive safe."

"Oh, you can count on it, Krissy. You have a nice holiday too. See yah." Jack picked up the envelope and headed toward the door. He turned and smiled at her. "Thanks for asking me to go to the concert with you. I really would have gone you know, if not for the holidays."

She nodded.

Jack felt pretty good as he stepped out into the cold air. Putting his sunglasses back on, he headed for his rig. If all went well, he should be back on the road in one half hour.

Jack chuckled to himself as he negotiated the maze of roads. Winter or summer, you were sure to find some kind of road construction here. He debated on stopping at the truck stop. They had a nice gift shop and he wanted to take something back for his sister. Nah, better get a move on. What with stopping to check the reefer controls so often, he wouldn't be making as good of time.

After putting in an audio book tape, Jack was on his way. As he drove past the Luverne exit, he was thinking, "Sometime I need go to Pipestone. A lot of Indian history around here."

Jack continued thinking about Pipestone. The American Indians had quarried the special rock to make their peace pipes from the earliest of recorded time. The area around the quarries was considered sacred and even warring tribes could come dig for stone without fear. During the 1930's the United States Government thought they could make some money off it and basically took it from the Indians. After finding out they couldn't make any money, they gave it back to the Indians. Now, only people of Indian nationality can remove the stone. This area is governed under the Park Service. The land around it is prairie grass and plants as it was in the1800's. There are paved walks so the handicapped people can tour the waterfall and quarry sites. Jack heard that one feels the Spirit when they are there. Some of the Indians make jewelry out of the stone and sell it. Then Jack laughed at himself. He was always going to take time to do something, but there were always the deadlines to get the load from one place to another.

I-90 was cleaned off pretty well. Here and there were cars and a few trucks in ditches. The land in this area was so flat, that the wind was constantly blowing snow across the road causing it to become icy from the heat of the tires. One had to keep his wits about him at all times. You never knew when you would hit a patch of black ice. At least he had a nice heavy load of meat in the back for traction. The company had just put all new tires on about two weeks ago and he had some good tread. Another gust of wind hit the truck about that time. Jack shut off the tape and turned on the CB.

He saw a truck coming from the east. "Hey Red Truck, got your ears on?"

"Yeah Reefer Man. How's it going?"

"Just pulled out of Sioux Falls, so far so good. Windy. How about you?"

"Man, the wind is blowing like crazy. Snow keeps drifting on the road. Only had about a foot of the darn stuff fell but there are drifts six and eight feet tall. Got a light load on and I've had to drop speed to keep the trailer behind me." The voice was that of an experienced trucker.

"I hear you man, the roads are pretty clean behind me, but still have that constant wind sweeping the snow across the plowed roads. The wreckers are starting to pull vehicles and a couple of trucks out of the ditches, so be prepared for them." Jack responded.

"Watch it; the bears are out in full force too, so there's a lot of action out there. I don't think they will catch too many for speeding today."

Jack laughed, "You forget, we have a lot of idiots out there and with the first good snow, they have to relearn how to drive. Ten four. Thanks, good buddy, and have a safe one."

Jack had no more than signed off when he could see in his left side mirror a car getting ready to pass him. Jack sighed. The driver was going way too fast for conditions. Jack started to mentally make a bet with himself on how long it would be before he passed the guy in a ditch. Jack was almost to the Worthington exit. Nope, the car didn't turn off. Well, he hoped whatever was so pressing was worth the risk the driver was taking. It was cold out and landing in a ditch with no heat could be dangerous. They tell you to stay with the vehicle, but it could be awhile before the highway patrol came through or someone stopped to help you. It was also dangerous to take a ride with anyone these days. Walking in the cold with the wind chill like it was equally dangerous. Cell phones really came in handy in these situations.

Jackson would be a good place to stop and take a break and check the reefer temperature. Funny, it was colder outside than inside the truck, but rules were rules. Next to the truck stop was a great restaurant connected to a motel that made fantastic meals from scratch. Omelets full of veggies, casseroles of all kinds, hearty soups, and homemade bread. Almost as good as his Mom's, *Almost*. The price was fair too. Of course there were some fast food places close by, but Jack avoided them like the plague unless he had to. All the fast food started to taste the same after awhile: cardboard with catsup on it.

The jake brake sounded as Jack signaled and slowly began the descent off Interstate 90. Luckily, the ramps were heavily sanded. He pulled into the truck stop and parked to the side. He checked his fuel gauge and saw that he had enough fuel to get to La Crosse. Jack decided to go to the restaurant across from the truck stop. He had eaten there many times and never had a bad meal. Reaching around for his jacket and hat, Jack figured he might as well get his log book up to date too. Leaving the truck running, he locked up. The minute he stepped in front of the truck the blast of arctic wind hit him. Turning up the collar on his coat, he made fast tracks for the restaurant.

The windows of the restaurant were steamed up, giving the appearance of a fairy land. Jack opened the door and stepped in and stamped the snow off his boots. The fragrance of soup and fresh bread assailed his nostrils. He wouldn't need a menu; Jack knew what he would be eating. He walked up to the counter instead of the tables. They always gave faster service for truckers. He wanted to eat and get back on the road. If he was lucky, he should be able to unload yet today and have the next three days off. He would be home in time for Thanksgiving.

The only other person at the counter was a young man about Jack's age. He was hunched over; his hands wrapped around a cup of coffee. He barely glanced at Jack when he sat down. No problem, Jack had a log to update anyway.

"What will you have young man?" The heavy-set, older waitress gave him a friendly smile.

Giving her a grin, "I could smell that wonderful soup and bread when I came in the door. How about a *big* bowl of the soup and a couple slices of bread. I would like a glass of milk too."

She smiled knowingly, "Yes, we make all our food here from scratch, and that does tend to give an inviting aroma to the air. Be right back, young man with your order."

Jack had completed updating his log book, when the waitress bought out his food. She stood back and watched as he started to eat with gusto.

"Good very good. Give my compliments to the cook." Jack told her.

"I'll do just that," she responded with a chuckle, turning toward the kitchen door.

Jack could feel the eyes of the young man looking at his food. He put the spoon down.

"When was your last meal?" Jack asked as he turned to face the young man.

"Yesterday. Someone lifted my wallet at the bus station. I live in Madison, but I can't reach my folks. If I could, I know they would wire me money to get home. It's way too cold to hitchhike, plus the State Patrol will give me a ticket if I get caught walking on the interstate. I'll try my folks again tonight. I don't know why someone isn't answering the phone. I'm really getting worried."

Jack waved to get the attention of the older waitress. When she came up to him, Jack said, "My friend here would like a big bowl of this delicious soup, the roast beef sandwich, and," he turned to the young man and asked, "Milk or a soda?"

"Milk, ah, milk will be just fine."

Facing Jack he sincerely said, "Thanks mister. I really appreciate this. My name is Mike by the way." Mike moved over to the seat next to Jack and shook hands with him.

The waitress set the food down in front of Mike and gave Jack a puzzled glance. She didn't see a total stranger buy someone a meal everyday. Neither one looked liked one of those funny guys, but then, you never can tell about people these days. She sniffed and left the counter area.

Mike made short work of the soup and started on the sandwich before he started to slow down on eating.

Jack grinned at him. "Need anything else?"

Mike smiled back. "No Sir, this was fine and if you give me your name and address, when I get home I'll send you some money."

"No need, just remember when you see someone else in this situation to help them. And for the record, don't call me sir. I save that title for my Dad." Jack reached in his pocket and pulled out his cell phone and handed it to Mike. "Why not try and give your folks another call."

Once more the young man's call went unanswered. His brow had a frown in it. "I don't know what to think. I tried my brother's place and no one answered there either. All I got was the answering machine again. Something terrible must have happened. Normally Mom would be busy in the kitchen with Thanksgiving dinner preparations." He handed the phone back to Jack with a sigh.

Jack punched some numbers into the phone. "Hi Frank, Jack O'Ryan here. No, no problems. Matter of fact, I'm not too far from home. Say, I ran into a friend of mine and want permission to let him ride to La Crosse with me." Jack was quiet. "Yes, I know I am supposed to get an okay in advance, but this just came up. Yes I have a form with me in the truck he can fill out. Yeah, thanks. Okay. You have a good Thanksgiving too." Jack put the phone back into his pocket.

"Mike, it looks like you have a ride to La Crosse with me and we can try and contact your folks from there. I have a form in the truck you need to fill out to not hold the trucking firm liable for anything. You ride at your own risk. Any problem with that?"

"No problem. Thanks Jack. I really appreciate this. I feel like I have been between that 'rock and a hard spot' people talk about." Mike mentally put this day's experience under his 'miracles do happen' folder.

Leaving a tip for the waitress, Jack picked up the bill and they headed for the cashier.

The waitress watched the two men as they went toward the door. She shook her head, 'made you wonder some days'.

Mike had a heavy backpack. Both men bundled up and stepped out into the bitter cold.

Once inside the truck, Jack had Mike put his backpack behind the passenger seat, and they shrugged out of their heavy coats. Jack found the form and Mike signed it without any hesitation. They put on their seatbelts, Jack checked all the gauges, and they were on their way. Barring any problems, they should be in La Crosse in no more than three hours.

The two young men chatted as the miles rolled by. They realized they had a lot in common, from food and music to the Green Bay Packers.

Lady Luck was on their side and Jack dropped off the trailer at the local company site and took the tractor over to the parking area. He plugged in the heater cord to the truck. Mike helped him load their things into Jack's personal truck.

Jack rented an efficiency apartment in town. This weekend, he would be staying at his sister's home since his folks and brother would also be staying there for the Thanksgiving weekend. He would do his laundry there, visit, and enjoy being off the road and with family.

When Jack pulled into the driveway, the front door burst open and there were his Mom and Dad, with big smiles on their faces. He got out and gave them big hugs. Mike had slowly followed behind.

"And who is this young fellow?" Jack's mom questioned with a warm smile at Mike.

Beckoning Mike forward with his hand, Jack introduced his parents to Mike.

"Hey, you guys, you're heating the outdoors, get in here." Deb, Jack's sister was pulling them into the house. "You want to catch your death of cold out there?"

Hugging his sister, Jack said, "Glad to see you too Sis. I want you to meet Mike. I met him on the road."

Laughing, Deb extended her hand to Mike. "I don't think there has been a year gone by that Jack hasn't brought someone home on a holiday. Welcome, Mike. Can we get you anything?"

"Oh, I'm not here for the holiday, although I appreciate the thought. I live in Madison. If I could use your phone, I'll try and contact my family again." Mike thought Jack had a friendly family.

"Sure, the phone is over there." Deb pointed at the desk.

First Mike tried his parents place. No answer. Then he called his brother's number again. On the fourth ring, "Hello."

"Kevin, it's me, Mike. Thank God I finally reached you! Where have you guys been? I've been trying to get a hold of you or the folks since yesterday."

"I just got in Mike. Bad news, Dad had a real bad heart attack. He was shoveling snow when it happened. We've all been at the hospital. Relax, he is going to make it, but it was nip and tuck there for awhile. We almost lost him. I only came home to shower and clean up. Then, I'm going back to take Mom home to rest and I'll stay with Dad. That's the only way she will go home and relax. She is worn out from worry and needs to sleep before she collapses on us. One in the hospital is enough. Where are you, Bro? We expected you home yesterday."

"Long story, Kevin. I got a ride to La Crosse with a nice trucker. Can you come and get me? The buses aren't running and I'm totally broke. Are you sure Dad is okay?" His concern showed in Mike's voice.

Jack had come up and over heard Mike's side of the conversation. He got Mike's attention. "No need for your brother to come here. My Dad and I will drive you home. Madison isn't that far."

"I can't ask you to do that; you've already done so much. My Dad had a bad coronary and they have been at the hospital all this time. That's why I couldn't reach anyone. Luckily, I caught my brother who had just come home to shower and change clothes."

Jack took the phone from Mike. "Hi, Kevin. This is Jack O'Ryan. Say, my dad and I will give Mike a ride to Madison. No need for you to spend time driving here. Sounds like you have your hands full."

After some more conversation, Jack handed the phone back to Mike and left him to talk with his brother.

Jack walked over to his father and put his arm around him. "Dad, I just volunteered you to ride shotgun with me to drive Mike home." Everyone was clustered around Jack listening to him. He relayed the information Kevin had shared. They all nodded their heads in agreement. It was the right thing to do.

Mike joined them. Everyone expressed sympathy for his dad's health.

Deb with her hands on her hips quipped, "When I heard Jack tell Dad they were taking you to Madison instead of having Thanksgiving here, I thought, 'my cooking isn't that bad'." Her small joke relaxed the group.

Deb and her mother herded the men into the cheery kitchen for lunch before they took off. There was playful banter as they got acquainted and enjoyed their food. They agreed, they would all be home for Thanksgiving tomorrow and they all had a lot to be thankful for.

CHAPTER 9

"Son," Bob said as he retrieved his winter coat from the closet, "I think we should take my car. It will be more comfortable than your truck, and it's all gassed up and ready to go. I'm even willing to let you drive my chariot, but mind you follow the speed limit.".

Jack laughed. "Pa, I know you mean well, but I feel safer when I am sitting higher in my truck than in your car. Plus, I have four wheel drive if we need it. Mike here," Jack gestured at Mike with his thumb, "Might find out when we get him home that the driveway isn't shoveled out and we may need the four wheel drive to deliver him right to the door. We wouldn't want him to get his feet wet." They all laughed.

"I didn't mean to start a family argument." Mike joined in with the camaraderie.

"No, you just don't understand my dear ole Pa here and his strategy." Jack put his arm around his dad. "He wants us to take *his* car, so five miles down the road he can put the seat back and sleep like a baby for a hundred miles or so in comfort. Of course, he'll be snoring all the way to make sure I don't fall asleep."

Bob O'Ryan started to sputter, "No respect from the young kids today, just *no* respect. Okay, okay. I give in. We'll take your truck. Don't know why I spoil you like I do." He shook his head, but his eyes were smiling.

Everyone said their good-byes to Mike and wished his father a speedy recovery.

The three men stepped out into the cold night. The stars were twinkling high in the dark velvety sky. There was a sense of peacefulness to the night as they walked to the truck, their warm breath making gray puffs in the air.

Mike elected to sit on the extended seat and let Mr. O'Ryan ride in front with Jack. He placed his overnight bag on the floor so there was room to put his feet up on the seat and stretch out if he wanted to. He was very weary, not having had a place to sleep the last couple of days.

He was worried about all the stress on his mom, and how she was coping with his dad's coronary. His parents were a very close and loving couple. He didn't need both parents in the hospital.

The truck idled while they put on their seat belts. Jack turned to his dad, "Pa, you have to promise me if you fall asleep you won't snore too loud. I didn't bring any ear plugs with me." Jack patted the truck seat. "You know these seats are pretty comfortable." Jack was chuckling.

Mike in the back waited for Bob to reply.

Bob turned around and put on a 'woe is me' expression, "Just like I said Mike, I get *no* respect, *no* respect." They all laughed and Jack backed out of the driveway.

Sharing experiences from their lives, the three men got acquainted as they covered the many miles.

Bob was a retired lawyer, but still kept a hand in the business as a consultant. He now had time for a few hobbies to fill up the time he had spent working. He and his wife did some volunteering and were active in their church.

Mike was going to medical school. After graduation, he would do his residency in the surgical field. Mike was fascinated and intrigued by the working of the human body. The miles sped by as he enthusiastically went into some of the realms of medicine he was studying.

"It is rather hilarious that no matter what disease we study, everyone thinks they have it." Mike said.

"You're going to have a problem when you get to the OB department." Jack laughed.

"No, I don't think I will be 'catching' any maternity problems." Mike responded with a chuckle.

They were going through the Wisconsin Dells area when the headlights of the truck picked up a car on the shoulder of the road. By the angle of the car, they knew something was terribly wrong. Only one of the car headlights was shining and that was very dim. Mike and Bob craned their necks to see as Jack slowed the truck down and pulled over behind the car. Jack put on the truck flashers. All three men got out to investigate.

One glance told the men the story. The car had hit a deer or the deer had jumped in front of the car too fast for the driver to avoid hitting it. The carcass was lying next to the car. The front windshield was shattered and blood and deer fur were everywhere. Jack opened the driver's door to find the driver unconscious with labored breathing, his hair and face red with blood. How much was from the driver and how much was from the deer was anyone's guess. If the young man hadn't been confined by his seat belt, he would have fallen on the snowy ground.

"Dad, go back to the truck and call 911 on my cell phone. Mike, under my seat you will find a blanket and the first aid kit. In the side pocket of the door, is a flashlight." Jack called over his shoulder as he tried to undo the seat belt so he couldn't ease the man back against the seat.

In no time, Mike was back with the blanket and first aid kit. They covered him up against the cold.

Bob soon joined them. "The ambulance is on the way. They said about five minutes. Luckily the mile marker is right here and I could give them our exact location. How is the young fella doing?" Bob held the flashlight as Mike took what vital signs he could. Jack cleared some of the fur out of the man's mouth and off his face, carefully checking for any embedded glass.

"His heart beat is steady, but his breathing is still labored. I think some of that deer's fur is lodged in his throat. I hope that ambulance gets here soon to suction him out. His face is cut and bruised, but it doesn't look like anything is broken. I can't tell about his eyes or his cheek bones." Mike spoke quietly.

In the distance they could hear the wail of the ambulance in the cold night air. It was a welcoming sound signaling help was on the way. Leading the ambulance was a state trooper, lights flashing on the squad car. The ambulance pulled up while the trooper situated his vehicle so no oncoming traffic would run into them.

The E.M.T.'s efficiently administered aid to the young man. They suctioned fur from his throat and he began to breathe better. Then they started an IV. The emergency techs worked in harmony. Once he was stabilized, they put a support collar around his neck and slid him onto the gurney and into the ambulance.

The four men stood watching the flashing lights of the ambulance as it got smaller and the loud siren faded as it sped toward a Madison hospital.

The trooper questioned them on what they knew about the accident. They all in turn gave their names, addresses and phone numbers and related what had transpired after they stopped. He thanked them for being good Samaritans, and told them to have a safe trip. Then he radioed for a wrecker.

Jack, his dad, and Mike gathered up the blanket and things and dragged the deer carcass off the road.

Back in the truck, they fastened their seat belts and Jack pulled onto the interstate.

"I've lived here all my life and this is the first time that I have come across a car/deer accident like this. I'm glad the ambulance arrived when it did. I was really concerned about his breathing and I didn't have enough knowledge or the instruments to open his airway if it was needed." Mike commented. "I didn't realize a deer that size could cause so much damage."

"Oh, I've seen some pretty bad accidents through the years," Bob remarked. "That's why I'm all for the deer hunting season. There aren't enough natural predators to keep the herds in balance and people who use the meat and like the challenge of the hunt prevent more of these incidents happening, or deer dying of starvation."

"I saw many deer carcasses along the roads earlier in the month." Jack interjected. "You always have to be on the alert. During the rutting season, the deer seem to throw caution to the wind. Early morning and late evenings they are out feeding. I'm surprised to see one at this time of night. Usually if you see one cross the road, you better be prepared for three or more to come bounding across. It's amazing the damage they can do to a vehicle. A lot of people have been killed. Imagine you are going 65 miles an hour and 100 to 264 pounds of sharp hoofs and horns come hurtling on to the hood, through the windshield into your vehicle and on your lap. And the people on motorcycles..." Jack didn't have to say anymore, they knew the answer.

They were discussing this and speculating on the injured young man when Mike leaned forward, "Take this exit Jack and at the stop sign, turn right."

Jack followed Mike's directions. Ten minutes later they were turning on the street where Mike lived.

"My house is the one with the yard light on, and look!" said Mike, "The drive-way is shoveled out. One of the neighbors must have done that. We have really great neighbors."

"Guess that means we don't drive you right up to the door Mike." Jack laughed.

As Jack pulled to the curb and shut off the truck, the front door opened and Mike's mom was silhouetted in the light.

"Mikey? Is that you?" She called out.

"Yes, Mom, it's me."

Mike stepped out of the truck and sprinted to the house and caught his mother in a big hug. They stood there, comforting each other in the silent embrace.

Jack and Bob got out of the truck. Jack reached back and picked up Mike's duffel bag then father and son slowly walked up the sidewalk to the house, giving mother and son needed time together.

Mike turned to face the two men, "Let's get out of the cold and into the warm house and I want you to meet my mom." He ushered them into the house.

"Mom, this is Jack, the man who came to my rescue and his dad, Bob O'Ryan. Gentlemen, my mother, Mary Kincaid." Mike finished the introductions.

"Thank you for bringing my son home. I can't tell you how much this means to me." A tear escaped from her eye. "It has been such a turmoil with my husband ill at the hospital and not being able to contact Mike." She started to weep again.

"Don't cry Mom, I'm here now. Kevin said Dad is going to be okay. Everything is going to be all right. We have so much to be thankful for this year." Mary nodded and rested her head on his shoulder. Gently they swayed together.

Bob cleared his throat. "I think we'll be heading back now. You two have a lot of talking to do." Bob understood things like this. "Besides, if we stay away too long, my son-in-law might try to sample those pumpkin pies by himself."

Mary put her hand on Bob's arm. "I won't hear of it Mr. O'Ryan. Why it's late and you two must be exhausted. I have plenty of room here. You can leave early in the morning."

"Dad's right Mrs. Kincaid, it's a holiday tradition for the men to sample one pie the night before. We can't let Joe and my brother Daniel eat our share. But we do thank you for your generous offer." Jack smiled warmly at her.

"You must let me pay you for bringing Mike all this way. I insist. This was so generous of you to help my son, especially on a holiday. Not knowing where Mike was and if he was okay and then finding out he was stranded, broke..." Mary paused and turned her head as the tears threatened once more to fall. Composing herself, "The peace of mind I received when I heard that Mikey was safe and on his way home...you'll never understand." She finished her sentence in a soft sob.

Bob took Mary's hands in his. "We wouldn't think of it Mrs. Kincaid. It was our pleasure to be of service." Bob said, and Jack nodded in agreement. Bob continued, "You folks just be all together and cheer up your husband. That will be thanks enough. Besides, meeting Mike made our circle of friends larger."

Father and son headed for the door. Mike caught up with them and shook first one hand and then the other. "This day has turned out much different because you entered my life, Jack. Of all the people who came into that restaurant, you are the only one who sensed I needed help. You are a very compassionate man, and I will never forget that act of kindness." Mike enveloped Jack in a big bear hug.

Bob stood back looking at the two young men, and he was very proud of his son. He and Alice tried to raise the kids to live a Christian life and do for others. Jack had received that message and was living it. He leaned back on his heels, yes; he was a proud and happy dad.

CHAPTER 10

It was a happy, relaxing Thanksgiving. Although it was Debbie and Joe's home, they had her dad sit at the head of the table. They bowed their heads as Bob gave the blessing for the meal and his family.

Jack peeked a glance around the table and felt a surge of love for his family. He felt truly blessed to be loved and nurtured by each of them. As his eyes stopped on Mira, his youngest niece, their eyes met and they smiled at each other.

Typical little six year old, she wanted to eat. She knew after the turkey and trimmings came the yummy pies. Grandma Alice had made special little pies just for her and Katie. Right before dinner Mira helped Grandma whip the cream for the pies and got to lick a beater afterward.

Uncle Jack kept saying, "Grandma is spoiling you, it's my turn to lick the beaters."

Grandma had replied, "Move out of the kitchen son. This is woman's work." Then she handed Katie the other beater to lick.

They all giggled as they heard Uncle Jack complaining to Grandpa. "Dad, mom won't let me lick the beaters. I'm sure it is my turn."

Grandma just laughed and whispered to the girls that men were just little boys in bigger bodies.

Back in the living room, "Jack, I seem to remember we all sampled a piece of pie last night." Bob replied, as he turned a page of the newspaper.

"Yeah, but it didn't have any whipped cream on it, so that didn't count." Jack countered.

Every one enjoyed the delicious meal. After they all had eaten too much food and shared many memories of happy times, the men retreated to the living room. Alice and Deb cleared away the leftovers. As much as the men wanted to vegetate after the meal, the little girls had other ideas and brought out some board games to play. Daniel thought they should watch the big football game on television but got out voted. And now the merry group around the dining room table were laughing and teasing as they played the games.

Deb and Alice enjoyed the music of laughter and gentle teasing coming from the other room as they loaded the dishwasher.

Jack checked in with dispatch and discovered he had to leave first thing in the morning. The company needed an order delivered by Monday morning. He hung up the phone in disgust! "Man, I just got home and wanted a few days with my family. One freeking day off! I was supposed to have a three day weekend. I don't even have my clothes washed. So much for spending time with the family. The life of a trucker. No life. Someone should kick me for checking in. I should have waited until Sunday night and checked with the dispatcher!"

"Hey Little Brother, cool down. Mom and I will do your laundry, fix up some sandwiches and put some pie and fresh fruit in containers. Mom has a whole week of meals froze for you to warm up in that oven you have. At least we have today together so quit complaining, be glad you have a job that lets you see America. Why don't you men take the girls and go for a walk and burn up some calories from all that pie you made disappear like magic." Deb made sense as usual.

Jack appreciated the fact that he had a caring family. And all he would have to do then was get some gallon containers of water for drinking. Now he felt a little embarrassed for spouting off.

Bob, Joel, Daniel, Jack, and the girls went for that walk before Alice and Deb thought of some chores they could do. Located a couple of blocks away, was a small neighborhood park. The men threw a Frisbee around and pushed the girls on swings. Then Jack and Daniel got into a small wrestling match. By the time they called it a draw, both young men were full of snow. Katie and Mira were laughing and calling them snow men.

"Snow men! Snow men! I think we need some snow girls." Jack and Daniel chorused. With that, each man picked up a niece and twirled them in the air and then rolled them in the snow. The girls squealed with delight.

"Hey Grandpa, how do you like our little snow girls?" Daniel asked his dad.

"I like them. How about we show the girls how to make snow angels?" Bob replied.

***

After the women finished doing Jack's laundry and the food preparation, they decided to get some fresh air too, and walked down to the park figuring the family would be there. They stood on the knoll and watched as four big men and two small girls lay in the snow moving their arms and legs back and forth to make angels. Mother and daughter smiled at each other and with a whoop and holler, slid down the slippery slope.

Reaching the family, Alice spoke up, "You call those angels? We'll show you how to make perfect angels." With that, both women found a spot, and proceeded to make a snow angel.

They all stood up and admired their angels, each one declaring their's was the best.

Laughing and holding hands, everyone covered with snow, they slowly walked up the snow packed hill and back to the house for some hot chocolate with marshmallows. Deb assured them there was plenty of pie and whipped cream to go with it.

Before they went into the house, they all brushed the snow off their coats and hats, and stamped their feet to knock snow off their boots. As they opened the door, the phone was ringing. Deb reached the phone first.

"Hello?" She listened and then looked at Jack, bending her index finger, beckoning him to the phone.

With a quizzical look, Jack took the phone from his sister. "Jack speaking."

"Hi Jack, Mike here. I don't want to disturb your Thanksgiving festivities, but my family and I are at the hospital and we were telling dad about all the help you and your family gave me yesterday and he would like to talk to you personally. Here he is."

The next voice on the phone was Calvin Kincaid. "Hello Jack?" Calvin's voice was steady and quiet. "I had to thank you for being a good Christian man. Mike told me how you came to his assistance and then went the extra mile and drove him all the way home. I don't know if you can understand how grateful I am to have my family around me at this time." There was a catch to his voice, close to a suppressed sob.

"No problem sir. I was glad to help. How are you feeling now?" Jack felt embarrassed by the call.

"Like I was driven over by that big black truck Mikey told me you drive." Calvin let out a soft chuckle. "Actually, the doc is telling me that I need a couple of bi-passes done and they have scheduled that for Monday. Gonna make a new man out of me, they say."

"That's great news Mr. Kincaid. Amazing what modern medicine can do. That means we'll all have had a wonderful Thanksgiving this year." Jack's voice was cheerful.

Once more the phone changed hands and Mary came on the line. "Jack, whenever you are in the Madison area, you be sure and stop. You and your family are always welcomed in our home. Thank you again for showing this act of kindness in our lives when we needed it. God bless your family."

"Thank you Mrs. Kincaid. Let me know how the surgery turns out. I'll be on the road, but if you call here, my sister Deb will relay the message. And don't worry. There are some highly trained doctors there." Jack was trying to reassure her.

They said their good-byes. Jack hung up and relayed the conversation to the family.

It had been a good day.

CHAPTER 11

Jack woke up to an overcast day. After he showered and dressed, he turned on the television to the weather channel. He watched a short time and groaned. He was going to be driving in bad weather the whole cotton pickin' way.

Deb came into the family room carrying a hot mug of tea. "What's the matter little brother?" She put her left arm around his waist and leaned her head on his shoulder. Jack hugged her back and took the colorful Thanksgiving mug from her.

"Smells good. Thanks Sis." Jack pointed at the television screen, almost spilling his tea. "Bad weather. Starting this noon around here and it will be with me all the way to Canada."

"Maybe you should wait until it passes. There isn't anything to deliver that is worth risking your life Jack." Deb voiced her thoughts aloud.

"You tell that to the dispatcher and the company who wants that order on their dock Monday morning. Besides, this is how I make my living Sis. Remember? When things get tough, just call on the truck drivers to keep things rolling. Hey, did I tell you I met a lady who called me a Warrior of the road? Pretty neat huh?"

"Okay, Jack. Spill. Who is she? Where did you meet her? Why did she call you a, what was that? Warrior of the road?" Deb was not taking no for an answer.

"When did you decide to become a newspaper reporter?" Jack laughed and headed for the kitchen. He sat down on a chair and reached for the newspaper.

"Oh no you don't! You're not getting off that easy!" Deb grabbed his arm. "Spill, or I call Mom and Dad and they're still sleeping."

"That's what you think young lady." Alice and Bob stood arm and arm in the doorway. They all had stayed overnight. "You heard your sister, spill. We're all ears Son."

Jack looked from one to another. He either had to 'spill' or he would never get any breakfast or be able to leave. Women. He related the story about Sara and her little boy Brian and how he gave them some road side assistance when the alternator broke on their car.

When he had finished, Alice came over and hugged her son. "I'm so proud to be your mother young man." She planted a kiss on the top of his head.

"Let's not make a big deal of giving a helping hand. I didn't do anything you wouldn't have done under the same circumstances. Now, is everyone going to talk all day or give me a nice breakfast so I can take off. I'm wasting away to nothing." Jack looked at his mom and sister with a 'cater' to me look.

After a nice family breakfast, Jack got his things packed and loaded in his personal truck. When he was done, he went back into the house. All the family were waiting to say goodbye.

Bob cleared his throat getting everyone's attention. "Will you all join hands and we will ask God to be with Jack and his truck as he travels." They bowed their heads and Bob prayed for his son, the rest of his family and the Kincaid family. He asked God to put a protective shield around the truck as Jack drove.

After many hugs, Jack left to pick up his semi and paper work at the yard. He stopped first and looked over his semi. He started it, and left it idling. Then he drove his pickup to the office area. He walked over to his box and picked up the envelope that told him what trailer he should hook up to and where he was going. He would also have the manifest papers that would tell him what check point he would be taking to enter Canada. He looked in the envelope. Oh great. This load was going to Rochester, New York where he would pick up a load of computers that would go to Canada.

In spite of the weather, Jack made pretty good time considering he was either in light snow, or a drizzle. Some areas had a lot of high wind. The traffic was pretty light and would be until Sunday night when the holiday travelers returned home. He saw a lot of deer tied to the top of cars too, so the deer hunters were successful.

He was getting tired and close to running out of hours, but the nearest service plaza had a bad reputation. They didn't patrol the parking lot to keep undesirable characters out of there like the good ones did. His eyes were tired from the strain of watching the road in the dreary weather. Jack was getting to the point he thought he would take his chances and stop.

Surprisingly, there were some choice spots yet to park in. Jack backed in and got ready to rest. He would keep the truck idling. It was too cold to shut the rig down and Jack didn't want to sleep in the cold either.

He had polished off one of the turkey sandwiches a couple of hours ago and wasn't hungry. Just tired. He thought he would amble up to the station, use the restroom and head back for some much needed sleep. He would fill out his log book in the morning.

Back in his truck, Jack crawled into the bunk, and picked up his book to read. He didn't even finish one page before his eyes kept closing. He shut off the light, rolled over and immediately fell into the deep sleep of a tired young man.

Jack woke up. He thought he heard something. There it was again. A tapping on his door. He ignored it. The tapping turned to a loud knock. Jack wondered who would be bothering him at this time of night. He stepped through the curtain, slid into the driver's seat, and looked out of the window.

There stood a young lady with way too much makeup on and long poorly bleached blond hair that came to her waist. She had on a dirty tan trench style coat with her arms wrapped around her waist. The wind kept blowing the hair into her face.

Jack didn't need to ask what she wanted. She was one of the lot lizards that this service plaza didn't keep out. He really had to put a sign on his truck that says 'No Lot Lizards'. He shook his head no and turned away.

She knocked on the door again. Jack turned back and rolled the window down a crack and growled, "What part of NO don't you understand? Get away from my truck!"

The lot lizard opened her coat and made sexual motions in the smallest bikini Jack had ever seen. He gave her a look of disgust.

"You can move on or I'm calling in a patrol car. You do understand English?" Jack spoke angrily. "You knock one more time on my door and I will open it to my pet Doberman who travels with me. He doesn't like strangers. Got it?" Jack rolled his window back up. Burr it was cold out there. She must be freezing standing there in her working clothes. White trash.

He crawled back into bed, and wondered if she believed his dog lie. Jack sure hoped so. He was tired. If he got woke up again, he just might buy a dog.

***

Relentlessly the rain pelted against the windshield. Thump, thump went the wiper blades as they darted back and forth across the window. Jack wasn't surprised at the weather. He just hoped the temperature didn't drop. The last thing he needed was the interstate turning into an ice arena. He kept the radio on to monitor the situation.

Jack was leaving Rochester, NY, going eastbound on the New York State thruway, headed for Syracuse. Jack slowed way down. It was too dangerous to go the speed limit in this down pour. The companies were closing and it was rush hour with bumper to bumper vehicles. Everyone was in a hurry to get home before the colder weather and snow came that the weatherman was forecasting. Jack groaned to himself, he wouldn't make any decent time with this weather. He was really weary of driving in these hazardous conditions. One day seemed the same as the next.

The headlights of the vehicles made the interstate look like the sky was on the ground. It reminded Jack of some outer space scene. Jack wondered what would happen if a flying saucer did land? Is there such a thing as a flying saucer? This weather was making him think weird thoughts.

Suddenly the rain hitting the windshield changed texture. Not quite snow, but not sleet, more of a mushy slush. Jack was getting off the road. His gut instinct told him it would get worse very soon. There was a service plaza entrance right here and he was taking it. In the few minutes it took Jack to pull off the road onto the lot, snow was falling so hard it he could hardly see. Be it Lady Luck or the angels, Jack wasn't sure, but he got the last parking spot. A few minutes later it was a total white out. You couldn't see a thing. It also made him think of the prayer his Dad offered up before he left home. How else you could explain his 'luck'?

Once more he mentally thanked his mom for making and freezing some meals for him. He put one in the warmer and listened to the radio. The report wasn't good. All along the 490 Interstate, were stranded motorists. They couldn't move. They couldn't see. The roads were shut down. Blizzard would be a good name for it.

Brave volunteer snowmobilers went up and down the road giving stranded people food and gas. Some truckers let people into their trucks to warm up. Greedy ones charged $50.00 to sleep in the upper bunk. Guess you could call them legal bandits. A few had some coffee and food in their trucks and of course, extra blankets. There wasn't much anyone could do but pray the vehicles didn't freeze up or run out of fuel.

Jack couldn't do anything to help so he went to bed knowing that his angels were watching over him and that back in La Crosse, his family had him in their evening prayers. It comforted him.

Jack woke to a strange feeling of being in an igloo. He couldn't see outside at all. He pulled on insulated coveralls, coat and boots. He hoped the doors of the cab weren't frozen shut. Armed with the long handled scraper and brush, he pushed open the door. A small avalanche of snow fell off the top of the cab onto his head. Jack was glad he had the hood on. He squinted his eyes against the glare of the sun reflecting off the snow, and reached back in for his sunglasses. As he cleaned off his truck, he joshed with some of the other truckers. "I think I am going to invent a nice big blower to clean off these rigs." Jack called out.

"Well, let me know when they are on the market, I want one." One of the other truckers answered back.

After some more kidding around and inspection of their trucks, they decided to go in and eat breakfast. They weren't going anywhere for a few hours minimum.

Some truckers were still sleeping and their trucks resembled odd blocks of snow.

They were starting to snowplow out the lot, but with the interstate full of stalled vehicles, it would be late morning before the roads were cleared enough for travel. Wreckers were out assisting some stalled cars, and a truck selling gas to motorists who had ran out of fuel idling their cars to stay warm. Jack had never seen anything like this before. The storm had hit so fast and furious.

CHAPTER 12

As long as he had time on his hands, Jack made good use of his cell phone. First he called his folks and sister to let them know he was okay. They always worried when he was on the road. Everyone was doing great. Mike had called the family and Calvin Kincaid came through the bi-pass surgery with no problems and should be released from the hospital by the end of the week. There was also a message for him to call Rosie.

The phone was answered on the second ring. The noisy back ground of the truck stop made it hard to hear. Jack asked for Rosie.

"Rosie speaking." Her voice had a nice quality about it.

"Hi, Rosie, Jack here. It doesn't sound like you. Mom said you called. Is everything okay?" She had never called him before.

"Yes, everything is fine. Just a minute. I'm going to put you on hold and pick up in my office. It's very hard to hear out here."

Jack heard the click. He counted to ten and Rosie was back on the line.

"Jack?"

"I'm here. You didn't lose me. What's up?"

"Well, I didn't know when you would be back out this way and I wanted to bring you up to date with Sara and little Brian. They stayed about a week with me and then she found a place she likes. She is house-sitting for a college professor that is on a six-month leave and all she has to do is pay for any long distance phone calls and their groceries. Would you believe it has four huge bedrooms and a den for the two of them! I really hated to see them go. Sara is so nice and that little Brian, what's not to like about him? He's a real charmer. Anyway, she will be taking two classes starting the first of the year. They have a day care there for Brian for those couple of hours so he can socialize with kids his age."

"The reason I called, Sara wants to send you a Christmas card. I know she has your cell phone number and could call you, but she doesn't want to seem forward. Is it okay if I give her your address? I thought I should ask you first." Rose respected his privacy.

"No problem, Kiddo. You can give it to her, and thanks for asking first. It's great to hear that they're making plans for the future. That little boy of hers was so quiet. So was she for that matter. I want to thank you again for taking them in. I know they could have gone to a motel, but when I asked you, I didn't know if she had any money or what her job prospects were." Jack's voice had a warm sound to it.

Rose laughed. "I guess the two of us are always on the lookout to lend a helping hand. Actually, Sara and I have become pretty close friends and they came over here and helped with the Thanksgiving Dinner we always give out free to the truckers. Did you know that she can play the piano? She had the guys singing and not feeling so alone away from family. Little Brian was really getting spoiled for the day. He loved all the attention. Sara has volunteered to help for the Christmas Dinner. I might take her up on it. I'm sure all the guys would enjoy having some homespun Christmas in the background. We were talking about her wearing a Mrs. Santa suit and dressing Brian up as a little elf."

Jack was smiling to himself with the image of the two dressed up for Christmas. "Well, it sounds like you two ladies have everything under control. How have you been, Rosie? Wished I had taken your advice that day and waited out the rain storm when I was there, but then, we never would have met Sara and little Brian." Jack thought a lot of Rosie.

"You're right about that, Jack. At the time I thought you were a wee bit nuts, but now that I think about it, maybe God had a plan and it was for you to be the one to help those two. As for me, I'm *fine* Jack. You know me, I'm always *fine*. Give me my hot cup of coffee and happy customers and I am not only *fine*, I'm GREAT! Say Jack, I'd like to give you my home phone number so we can keep in touch. I don't like to call you on your cell phone or bother you, but when you have some sit-and- wait time, give me a call." Rosie gave him her home number and they hung up. No one ever had enough *good* friends.

Jack shut off his phone. It looked like he could finally get a move on. It was almost noon. The traffic was moving slow, but at least it was moving.

Taking highway 81 north from Syracuse, Jack headed toward Ogdensburg where he would switch to highway 37 and cross over at Cornwall into Ontario, Canada. Jack couldn't travel with much speed on the two lane winding, hilly, roads. But it was a pretty peaceful drive. It reminded him of good ole Wisconsin.

As Jack pulled into the truck lane at the Cornwall check point, he was wondering how long this would take. Sometimes they went through the truck with a fine tooth comb and even made you unload the truck. Other times they only checked the manifest papers. You never knew. Jack wasn't worried. His company went back and forth a lot and was always completely legal, so if they recognized the driver, and by looking at the manifest recognized both company and driver as legitimate, he didn't get much hassle.

Jack let his truck idled and waited his turn.

The customs agent asked him to step down from the truck and bring his packet of papers: then they walked to the back of the semi. Not only was the trailer locked, but there was also a seal applied when Jack had picked up the load of computers. The agent checked out the numbers and went back to the cab of the truck. He climbed in and looked around, under the bunk, in the small refrigerator and even in Jack's duffel bag. Getting out, he asked Jack to take out everything he had in his coat pockets. Satisfied with his quick search that there weren't any weapons or drugs, he let Jack go through. The stop had taken half an hour.

Pulling slowly away from the check point, Jack decided to treat himself to a motel room for the night. Thankfully, he had been here before and knew where to go. Unlike the United States, Canada didn't have a lot of billboards or road signs. One good thing, they all had electric hook-ups for the vehicles, something the United States could do. Jack parked in the far end of the lot so the engine noise wouldn't bother anyone, and would let his semi run for the night. He didn't want to take the chance of plugging it in and the weather getting too cold and the truck not starting.

He carried his bag into the motel and got a room as far away from the elevators and ice machines as possible. The young lady spoke English with a French accent, and gave him the trucker's discount. Jack got his receipt so he could turn it in to the company and get reimbursed. Tonight he was going to relax, maybe watch a movie, but first, a shower and some dinner. Across the street was a restaurant known for serving very great tasting seafood.

After Jack finished eating, he strolled through the small picturesque town, thinking he might find a few Christmas presents for his family. He looked, but didn't find anything special. But then, he really wasn't in a shopping frame of mind. Walking back in the cold night air, the snow crunching underfoot, Jack felt a little lonely. In his mind he visualized his family back home, busy with their nightly routines. He thought of Rosie, Krissy and Sara. Yah, he felt lonely tonight. Then he looked up at the stars in the skies and thanked God for his family, many friends, for his health and for his safety on the roads, especially through the blizzard in New York. Then he felt better, no longer alone.

The warm air of the lobby felt good as Jack opened the door. He wiped his boots on the mat to remove the snow and looked around.

Many of the people staying there were gathered in the lobby. It was more of a visiting time. People came out of their rooms, read the paper, played some cards, much different than in the States. He could hear the lilt of the French language and some English. The scene reminded him of an old Rockwell painting from the *Saturday Evening Post*. Just as he decided to see what videos were available at the desk, the door opened and four young men came tramping in from the cold, carrying instrument cases. Jack perked up, wondering who they were and what would transpire. He hadn't played his guitar with others in a long time. He watched and listened.

The young receptionist stepped from behind the desk and greeted the four young men warmly in French. She walked to the middle of the room, clapped her hands to get everybody's attention. "Monsieurs and Madames. My frere and his college friends will give a small concert in the next room for those who would like to listen, sing along, dance or join in with the music. There is no charge for this. They want to share some Christmas spirit early."

Jack quickly changed his mind on the video and followed the group into the other room. There the wooden floors were bare, no rugs except by the fireplace that had a cheery fire burning. Three of the young men took their instruments out and let them warm up. The fourth young man went to the piano, and ran through a series of warm-up scales. There were couches and chairs that the audience sat on. The rest stood in small groups visiting.

The music started, and soon the requests came in. Some people stood around the piano to sing, others danced. Jack knew a few tunes and joined in. He was really lost though when they sang totally in French. Then he hummed along and tapped his foot to the beat. It was a delightful evening. After about an hour of singing, the desk clerk entered the room, pushing a trolley cart with hot chocolate and cookies on it. Everyone stopped and partook of the tasty refreshments. When the four men picked up their instruments after the short intermission, Jack gave them a wave and headed for his room. Tomorrow would come early and he needed some shuteye. It had been a nice restful evening.

* * *

Jack woke up to the phone ringing. Automatically he reached for it. "Hello."

"Ah *bonjour*, Monsieur Ryan. It is your wake up call, eh?" The desk clerk spoke so cheerfully.

Jack had forgotten he had asked them to wake him up. "*Oui*. Yes, thank you."

"We have coffee and delicious warm croissants downstairs. *Oui?*"

"Yes. Thank you very much. I will be down shortly." Jack's voice was still groggy with sleep. He flopped back on the bed and shut his eyes, trying to remember where he was and what day it was. Slowly he opened them and looked at the sunshine making light dancing shadows in the room. He was in Canada and it was Monday morning and he had a load of computers to deliver in...he glanced at his watch, one hour.

Jack got up, jumped into the shower and shaved. After he dressed and put his things back into his bag, he left a tip under the pillow and went downstairs for some coffee and freshly made croissants.

* * *

Slipping on his sunglasses, Jack stepped out into the crisp, sunny morning. He paused and inhaled a deep breath of air. It was a good morning to be alive. The snow crunched under his boots as he walked toward the semi. It reminded him of a scripture that someone had put to music, "This is the day that the Lord hath made, let us be glad and rejoice."

Unlocking the door to the truck, he set his bag in and went back out to check the tires, lights and other things. Stepping up into the cab, he also looked at his dash controls and computer and turned up the heater. It was a wee bit chilly in there. He put his things away and slid into his driver's seat. Putting on the seatbelt, he shifted the big rig into gear and checking both side mirrors, was on his way.

The ten minute drive went quickly. Jack had delivered to this company before. He expertly maneuvered the truck into position at the dock. After so many years of driving, he very seldom had to take more than one try to back the truck anywhere. It was as though he and the truck were one. To non semi-drivers, this skill seems like an art to have such control over the huge truck.

Jack grabbed the manifest envelope and climbed down from the cab and headed for the side door where the warehouse office was located. The manager would check the papers and then they would both watch and count as the trailer was unloaded. When all the boxes were accounted for, the manager would sign and date the papers. From there, Jack went to the front office where they took their copy and transferred the funds immediately to the company.

As Jack opened the front office door and stepped in, he almost dropped his envelope as he was caught in a big bear hug

"*Bonjour* Monsieur Ryan! Welcome again to our wonderful city!" Pierre's booming voice gave a hearty welcome.

"Thanks, Pierre. I'm glad to see you too! What are you doing here? You told me on my last trip that you were going to retire." Jack patted the older gentleman on the shoulder.

"Ah, le company wishes for me to wait for the end of the year. It is good. Momma, she is getting ready for Christmas and it is 'Pierre, do this. Pierre, do that'." Pierre raised both arms and let them drop to his side. "It is easier to work here. I think I may not retire at all. Eh?" Then his deep laugh started to rumble. Everyone knew Pierre loved his wife dearly and was ready for retirement.

Pierre looked at his watch. "Monsieur Jacques, it is almost noon. You are done here, *oui*? We go to lunch. You come home now with me. Momma has big kettle of soup simmering, some freshly baked bread, some wine? Ummm." Pierre kissed his finger tips and then gestured up in the air with a contented look on his face.

"Yes, lunch would be fine, but I don't want to be any bother, Pierre. No wine though. I'm driving you know." Jack knew what a fantastic cook Annette was. He didn't care what she cooked, it would be delicious. Pierre had taken him home once before when he got in too late to get unloaded for the day. It was a warm, happy home.

"Mon Cherie would scold me if she knew you were here and I didn't bring you home. We go now." Pierre took Jack by the arm and marched him to the door. He stopped, turned around, and spoke to the secretary. "We will be back after Momma feeds my American friend."

The men got into Pierre's old car for the short ride. He lived about three miles away in a secluded farm setting. The old house had been in the family for over a hundred years, quaint, but charming. The rambling but sturdy cottage was a mixture of stone and wood that had been added onto over the years and well maintained.

Jack could see the smoke rising from the chimney and swirl around the top of the roof as they approached. He felt strangely like coming home.

They stamped the snow off their feet, stepped into the enclosed back porch, and took off their boots. As they open the door and entered the kitchen, the wonderful aroma of beef and barley soup filled the air.

"Momma! Look who I brought home. Monsieur Jacques!" Pierre's booming voice filled the charming kitchen.

Annette, a grandmotherly lady, came out of the pantry with a huge loaf of bread in her arms. Seeing Jack, her face beamed with a smile. Setting the bread on the table she reached out her hand to shake his. Instead, Jack raised her hand to his lips and kissed it.

"Madame Goncourt. You're lovely as ever. Pierre insisted I come for lunch. I hope you won't mind the intrusion," Jack took a deep breath, "Oh my. The fragrance of the soup is so wonderful; the taste will be fit for a king." Jack's stomach let out a huge growl sound and they all started to laugh.

"You are always welcome in our home, Monsieur Jacques. We are honored to have you. Now, you and Papa wash your hands while I set the table for my two kings." Annette ordered in a friendly manner.

The two men headed for the long, old, kitchen sink and washed up. They were just drying their hands on the towel when a black haired young beauty came bursting into the room. Seeing Jack, she came to an abrupt stop. Never taking her eyes off Jack she spoke to her father.

"Oh Papa! You have brought me an early Christmas present. *Oui*? I like him." Louisa slowly circled Jack like a cat ready to pounce.

Pierre and Annette spoke sharply in unison. "Louisa! Behave! Sit down".

Her big brown eyes danced and she had a secretive smile on her face. Louisa never took her eyes off Jack as she slowly slid into her chair.

Jack assumed it must be her usual place to sit.

Pierre and Annette were deeply embarrassed by their daughter's forwardness. Jack just stood there not knowing what to think as Louisa kept fluttering her eye lashes at him.

Flustered, Pierre turned to Jack and began to apologize profusely for his daughter's rude behavior.

"Momma and I send her to college and she loses all her manners. I shall send her to her room without lunch, then maybe to the convent for the nuns to pray for her." Pierre threatened.

Jack shook his head no and he was smiling. He actually thought this was all pretty funny and was having a hard time not laughing. He could see that Louisa was teasing, but Pierre and Annette were still old-fashioned and totally embarrassed by their daughter's actions. He could feel his face getting red and was afraid he would burst out in laughter and then the two older people would send him off without any lunch either. King Jack would be dethroned.

"I don't think this young lady would want me for Christmas. I don't do any tricks and I have to be fed three times a day, but I am house broken." Then Jack couldn't hold it in anymore as chuckles escaped then escalated in to full blown laughter.

They all looked at each other and laughed with him. The tension was broken.

"Monsieur Jacques, my naughty daughter Louisa. Louisa, our guest, Monsieur Jacques O'Ryan."

Louisa got a stricken look on her face. "Not *thee* Jacques O'Ryan?"

Pierre and Annette's gray heads were bobbing up and down in accord.

"Oh my gosh! I am so sorry to tease. You are le Jacques who saved my Papa's life." Louisa sprang from her chair and was clutching Jack's arm, tears streaming down her face. "I would never insult you. Is there anything I can do for you, Monsieur O'Ryan? I thought you were one of my brother's friends, and I just meant to tease since he always embarrasses my friends."

* * *

The last time Jack had delivered a shipment here, Pierre had been outside by the railroad track at the far end of the parking lot. He was cleaning some debris away from a switch. Somehow, he slipped and his foot got caught.

Jack had been catching up on his log while waiting to be unloaded when something caught his eye and he looked up. He saw Pierre struggling to free his foot, when he felt a chill run down his back. There was a train coming. If Pierre didn't get his foot loose, he would be killed. The adrenaline kicked in. Jack flung open the door and leaped out of the cab. He started running fast the minute his feet hit the ground. He prayed as he sprinted across the parking lot, "God, let me get there in time! Help me!"

Pierre saw the tall American charging across the huge lot and glanced back at the approaching train. He didn't want to die. Not yet. Suddenly there was a lot of shouting as the other men realized what was happening and they all raced toward the railroad tracks to assist.

In the distance Pierre could hear the whistle of the train and the squeal of brakes being applied. A cold sweat of fear broke out all over him. He had never felt so afraid or helpless.

Jack came to a sudden halt as he reached Pierre scattering small rocks and dirt. A glance showed the boot was twisted and caught between the iron track and wood tie. He grabbed Pierre's leg and pulled on it. Jack was afraid a bone might break, but better broke than dead. Bracing himself, Jack gave the leg one more hard pull and the foot came free from the boot. Pierre was a big man, but somehow Jack pushed or rolled, none of them really remembered how, and they were off the track, just in the nick of time, as the threatening black engine screeched by, not coming to a complete stop for another whole block.

Jack was half lying on Pierre, not moving, as they sucked in some deep breaths of air, realizing what a close call they had. Men began pounding Jack on his back, congratulating him for saving their friend. Others were checking over Pierre, especially his foot, wondering if anything was broken.

Running down the side of the track were the engineer and others from the train. The engineer's face was chalk white. When the engineer realized what was happening on the tracks, his stomach knotted in fear as he'd tried desperately to stop the iron monster.

He looked over at what was left of the mangled boot, thankful that it didn't contain a foot. Breathless in French, he inquired as to the welfare of Pierre and how it happened. "I felt so helpless when you didn't respond to my warning whistle. There was no way I could stop ze train in time. I thought you both were dead. Mother of God, you are alive." He made the sign of the cross.

Following suit, each man in the way of his religion, also thanked God for saving Pierre.

In the distance, the sound of a siren was getting louder as the ambulance pulled into the parking lot with its lights flashing, siren blaring before coming to a screeching halt by the group of men. One EMT got out of the vehicle carrying a medical bag and hurried to Pierre who was now sitting up. After examining his ankle and foot, they assumed it was badly sprained, but not broken. They wanted to take him to the hospital for an x-ray, anyway

"I am fine. I don't need to go to the hospital. Here, give me a hand up." Pierre was protesting loudly. "I just need to get off this cold ground."

"Pierre, you need to have them x-ray your foot and leg. First to make sure there isn't any hairline fractures or muscle tears." Jack was still kneeling on the ground next to Pierre.

"I am strong man. Big like bull. Momma will soak my foot and it will be good as new. See, no bones sticking out. Some new boots and all is well." Pierre looked up at everyone trying to convince them as well as himself.

"How about I go with you for the check-up? Besides, both your company and the train investigators will need a report to make sure everything is okay." Jack said in a quiet voice.

Pierre looked around at everyone. He didn't see anyone looking at him as though he was a weak man. He couldn't take that. A broken foot, *oui*, but not pity, and young Jacques did make sense.

"We go then," Pierre declared. Everyone gave a sigh of relief.

And that is how Jack became a hero in the Goncourt household.

* * *

Annette went to her daughter and hugged her. Pierre blew his nose and Jack, well Jack heard his stomach rumble again. In fact, everyone heard his stomach rumble again. There was a small flurry as the women put the soup and fresh bread on the table, and Pierre got Jack seated. They joined hands and Pierre offered a blessing over the meal and for the man who saved his life. And they had a wonderful meal and camaraderie.

Once again, Father Time dictated that Jack had to leave. They all walked to the door and Pierre and Jack shrugged on their winter clothes.

Jack turned and hugged Annette. "Thank you, dear lady, for having me in your home. Your food was excellent. I think you should start up the 'Annette Restaurant'. Then you'll have *real* kings sitting at your table."

"Monsieur Jacques, you are too kind." She hugged him back. "You and Pierre are the only kings I need in my home."

Then Jack turned to Louisa, "Next time I come, I'll remember to wrap myself up in Christmas paper and red ribbon."

Louisa blushed and they all laughed. "*Abientot* Monsieur Jacques, *aurevoir*." Both women called out. Mother and daughter stood and continued to wave, until the old car vanished down the narrow lane to the road.

It had been another good day with friends.

CHAPTER 13

Jack made it safely back to Wisconsin and picked up his next load. Destination: California. He was hoping they would have kept him closer to home. He needed to get some Christmas shopping done and the weather was terrible, the worst winter Jack had driven in since he became a semi driver. It seemed like every three days it was more snow and cold. Well, once he got over the mountains, California would be easier driving.

He glanced again at the paper work. Hey, he would be going through Woodland again. He would get to see Rosie, Sara, and little Brian. He made a mental note to stop at a mall and pick up some Christmas gifts for them. He thought Brian would like a big red truck of some kind.

But then he thought at The Shasta National Forest gift shop they had replicas of the second highest volcano in the Cascade Range with lights that made it look like lava flowing over the sides. Nah, maybe a toy duck or geese that the Sacramento Wildlife Refuge sold Brian would like better. They usually had wind up ones that made noise. That would keep him entertained and they could talk about the ducks that wintered at the refuge.

The trip was uneventful and the weather was cold but at least not snowing.

He had a horrible headache and he had felt achy for the past two days. He coughed again. His chest was congested and his breathing was becoming labored. Jack alternated between sweating and freezing. His throat was on fire. His arms felt like lead weights. Then he got another coughing spasm. He caught his breath and took a drink of tea. He wished he had some of his Mom's homemade chicken soup. That always made him feel better, and he felt terrible.

About two hours away from Woodland, Jack took another sip of water. Maybe if he kept sipping, his throat wouldn't hurt so much. All he wanted to do was shut down, crawl into his bunk and sleep, but he kept driving, his goal Woodland.

Finally he was going past Elvaton, CA which was about three miles from the truck stop Rosie and Carl owned.

He punched in Rosie's number on the cell phone.

"Hello." Her voice sounded so far away.

"Rosie, this is Jack. I'll be pulling into the truck stop in minutes if I can hold on. I don't know what is wrong with me." Another fit of coughing stopped his words. "I've never felt this sick before I'm having trouble breathing."

"Jack, can you make it? Stop the truck. I'll bring over a driver to bring it here. Jack? Jack! Answer me!" Fear was in her voice.

The sound of the cell phone dropped on the floorboard sent shivers through her. She felt utterly helpless.

Looking up Rosie saw the big black rig Jack drove slowly pull in the driveway and stop dead center in the middle of the parking lot. She slammed down the phone and yelled at two drivers eating at the counter, "Come with me! There's a sick driver out there that needs help."

The two men looked at each other, slid off their stools and followed Rosie who was racing to the truck.

She hiked up her skirt in order to step up, and opened the door, receiving the shock of her life. Jack was slumped over the steering wheel. Only God knew how he found the strength to shift the truck into park.

"Oh my God! Call an ambulance now!" Rose called out. "Jack, Jack, what's the matter?" She touched his forehead. It was burning hot and his breathing was labored. He never responded.

In minutes, the ambulance pulled up next to the truck. They struggled but got the unconscious young man out of the truck unto a gurney and into the ambulance. Jack was headed for the hospital.

Rosie had one of the truckers back the semi into a spot. She took out the packet that held the invoices. Locating the companies number, she called them, explaining what had transpired.

They asked if she could find a driver to finish the delivery and bring the truck back to her place. When Jack was better, they would find a load for him to bring back. Would she keep them apprised of Jack's condition, and if he needed anything to let them know.

Entering the busy kitchen of the truck stop, Rosie talked to Carl, her partner explaining what was happening. He understood. They were discussing which driver to ask to deliver Jack's load, when Lou came striding into the building. Rosie knew that Jack and Lou were friends and Jack had immense respect for Lou and the way she handled her rig. Rosie couldn't think of anyone better to take this load than Lou if she had the time.

"Lou, Lou. May I have a word with you?" Rosie asked in excited tone as she swiftly approached the older woman.

"Why sure young lady, what can I do for you?" Lou answered leaning one arm on the counter, her cigarette dangling out of the left side of her mouth.

"The ambulance just took Jack to the hospital. I don't know what's wrong with him. Somehow he managed to get into the lot and stop the truck before he passed out. I'm going there right away. Can you finish his delivery? There are just two stops. I talked with his dispatcher and they asked me to find someone we could trust. He said he will pay you the same as what Jack gets. We can go over that later. I know there isn't anyone but you that Jack would trust with his rig. Will you?"

Lou straightened up fast when she heard Jack was ill. She snuffed out the cigarette and grabbed the brown envelope out of Rosie's hand. "These the papers?"

Rosie nodded, and handed her the truck keys.

"Don't fret none, Rosie Girl. That boy is a good friend of mine. I'll make these stops and be back to see him. When he wakes up, you tell him that." Lou blew her nose. Dang, she was getting soft.

Rose gave her a big hug. "Just a minute, Lou. Let me give you my cell phone number." Rosie scribbled the number on an ordering ticket. She also wrote one meal on Rosie. "Show this to one of the girls when you order your meal. Make it a nice, thick, steak. It's on the house. I have to get to the hospital now."

Both ladies hurried for the door, each on her own mission.

On the way to her car, Rose punched in Sara's number and explained about Jack.

"I'll ask the neighbor to watch Brian. I don't want him there until we know how Jack would be. I'll meet you there." Sara hung up the phone.

* * *

Sara paused at the door, watching the nurse and Rosie at the bedside. Sara felt fingers of fear clutch at her chest. She wrapped her arms around herself. Jack was lying there so still. She wondered what happened to the strong man who had helped her and Brian.

The thin older nurse stopped adjusting the IV tubing and turned to leave. Reaching the door, she asked in a unfriendly voice, "Are you a relative of Jack's?"

Shaking her head slowly Sara said in a soft whisper, "No. No, I'm just a friend. How is he doing?"

The nurse gave her a weird look. That was the same answer the young lady at the bedside said. 'Just a friend'. What kind of guy was he? He looked clean cut, but then, the other lady said he was a trucker. The nurse sniffed in a superior way. Um, probably a rowdy man. She leaned closer to Sara. "Normally we don't tell anyone but family, but since his family isn't around...he is a very sick man. He has a severe case of bronchial pneumonia and is very dehydrated. We are giving him medication intravenously with fluids to help hydrate him." With that, the aloof nurse exited the room.

Sara sidled slowly over to the bed. Rosie took her hand and squeezed it. Sara's face was chalk white.

"Sara, are you okay? You aren't going to faint on me are you? I don't think the bed is big enough for the two of you and floor doesn't look very soft and comfy to me."

Sara gave a wan smile at Rosie's attempt at humor.

"I guess I wasn't prepared for this, you know, Jack so very ill like this. The last time I was in the hospital was to identify my in-laws." Tears welled up in her eyes.

Rosie gathered Sara in her arms. "Oh Sara, don't be so scared. Jack will be fine. We just need to get him through this pneumonia. He's going to need a place to stay when he gets discharged. What do think of him going to your place to convalesce? I really can't take off work right now, or I would take him home."

"I would be happy too. Anything for Jack. Brian will be tickled to have him there too. Did the doctor say anything to you about Jack's illness?" The color was slowly returning to Sara's cheeks. Being needed to her meant Jack wouldn't die.

"Just that it was a wait and see for right now. Jack is young and strong. I hate to leave, but I need to get back to work. Now that you are here to be with Jack, I just don't want him being alone. I also plan on calling his folks. I have his sister's phone number and she can relay the message to them. I do think they need to know now. Is it okay if I give them your home phone number and address? Oh, I have Jack's billfold. I needed to find out his insurance information for the hospital. I also notified his employer. Lou stopped in and agreed to deliver Jack's drops and return the truck to the lot. This was per instructions from his boss. Be sure and tell Jack this if he wakes up and is worried about the truck and cargo. We don't want him to stew about it. We need to keep him quiet so he can rest and recuperate." Rosie smiled at Sara.

"Sure, give his folks my phone number. They are welcome to stay at my place if they want to come out. I have the extra room. You might want to give them the phone number for this room too. Shoo, get going. I'll be here and I promise to call you if anything unusual happens." Sara gave Rosie a hug.

Rosie leaned over, tenderly kissed Jack on the forehead, and with a wave at Sara, left.

Sara set her brown purse and jacket on the chair next to the bed. Why were all hospital chairs the same: cold, and uncomfortable? Leaning over the bed, Sara gently touched his forehead. It felt so hot. Sara wondered if she should put a cold washcloth on his head or not. Sara decided she would wait until the nurse came back into the room and ask her. She slid her hand down the length of his arm and rubbed his hand that lay so still on the top of the crisp white sheets. She thought of how he came to her rescue, her 'warrior of the road'. Funny, how she instinctively had trusted him, a total stranger that dark raining night. Now, she could repay his kindness. For the first time since Jimmy had died, she finally felt alive. It felt good to be needed again.

Pulling the chair closer to the bed, Sara sat down and sent up prayers on Jack's behalf. It was the only thing she could do now.

CHAPTER 14

Jack was floating in a cloud and it was very comforting except for the elephant sitting on his chest. He felt a cool hand touch his forehead. *It must be an angel for sure. Maybe he'd died and gone to heaven. Was heaven like a cloud? He thought there should be music; angels singing or something like that? Funny, he didn't hear any harps or trumpets. Perhaps Gabriel lived on the other side, not by Peter and the Pearly Gates.*

Something was resting on top of his right hand. Maybe he should open his eyes and look. He tried, but his eyelids were just too heavy. He lay very still, trying to absorb his surroundings. His left arm felt cold and stiff. Once more he tried to take a peek. His eyelids fluttered up and down a couple of times before they stayed open.

What happened to heaven? Where did it go? Jack didn't recognize the room that was lit by a small floor lamp. The curtain was drawn and Jack assumed that it was night. "*No, I guess this isn't heaven.*" He wondered where he was and why he was in bed and not in his semi.

Looking down to see what was holding his right hand, he was very surprised to see a ladies' hand on his. The lady had fallen asleep, and her blond head was resting on the bed. His first thought...it must be Sara. His second thought, no, it can't be. Why would Sara be here? He closed his heavy eyes again and relaxed into the pillow. He sighed. Maybe he could get back on that cloud, find out who was in charge of music.

A bout of coughing shook Jack out of his relaxed state as he struggled for some breath.

"Jack! Oh Jack! Are you okay? Should I get a doctor?"

Jack's eyes flew open at the sound of Sara's concerned voice. He shook his head and lay back down, exhausted by the coughing spell. Once more he felt Sara's cool hand rub his brow. It felt good. Sara was here. Sara must be an angel.

For the first twenty-four hours that Jack was so ill, Sara and Rosie took turns staying with him. Lou also came by and sat with the young man. Once she knew he would be okay, Lou headed out with her load. She wanted to be back in Missouri for Christmas with little Momma and the rest of the family. It had been a *very* long time since she had a place to go on Christmas. For once, she wouldn't be alone for a holiday.

In the meantime, Rosie had contacted Mr. and Mrs. O'Ryan. Since it was so close to Christmas, and the idea of Jack being well enough to drive home was out of the question, Rosie invited the family out to Woodland. This included Jack's brother, Daniel, and his sister Deb and her family. Between Sara and Rosie, they would have the family stay with them. The family said they would help with the Christmas dinner at the truck plaza. As soon as arrangements were made they would all be flying out.

Jack was well enough not to have someone with him round the clock. Sara had just left and Rosie was visiting.

"Rosie? Can I ask you another favor?" Jack spoke in a quiet, slow voice.

"Sure, Jack. What is it?" Rosie never hesitated. He wouldn't ask her if it wasn't important.

"Do you have time in your busy schedule to pick up some Christmas presents for me? I don't even have enough energy to order any over the phone with my credit card. I need a gift for Sara, Brian and all the staff on this floor. What do you think?

"No problem Jack, but you might want to increase that list. I was going to keep this as a surprise, but your folks, brother and sister and family are flying in to be with you on Christmas. Your mom, dad and Daniel will stay with me. Deb, Joe, and the girls will stay with Sara and Brian. We were originally going to have you stay with Sara since I work, but with your folks coming...you can stay at either place!" Rosie was so excited. "Not only that, but your family has agreed to help out with the Christmas dinner and program for the truckers. Guess you have to be well enough to play that guitar of yours. What better instrument than a guitar to play '*Silent Night*'?

Jack felt moisture filling his eyes. How did he ever get so lucky to come across such nice people? And his whole family, to leave tradition behind and fly out to be with him during this time, he was one lucky man.

The two made a list of presents that Jack wanted Rosie to shop for. It didn't take long, but Rosie saw that Jack was already getting tired.

"Jack, I think I better leave and get started on this list. I am really excited about Christmas. My family is so scattered, it will be like having a family Christmas when yours arrive here." Rosie clapped her hands with glee. "Now my friend, you take a nap until your lunch comes. I'll stop back later and let you know how my shopping expedition went." She patted his hand and leaned over and kissed the top of his head.

Jack lay back with a sigh. He hated to see her go, but he was so tired. All that planning had exhausted him. He closed his eyes as she walked out the door. He was following orders. If Rosie had turned and walked back to the bed, she would have found him already enfolded in the arms of slumber.

* * *

If Rosie thought she was excited, then Sara was exhilarated! She purchased Christmas decorations for the house, made sure all the rooms were ready, put in a supply of groceries and bought some presents for everyone that would be there. She was waiting to buy the tree until the family came. It would be something they could all do together. She checked

Professor Green's music and found a wonderful assortment of Christmas arrangements. She was ready.

Sara planned on putting Jack in the den. She had a bed put in there. This way he would be downstairs with all the action, but he could still close the door when he wanted to rest. She wondered about how much rest he would get with Brian and his two nieces racing around.

Jack's sister Deb had called numerous times. She was shipping everyone's gifts out UPS. They were planning on renting a van when they got there and would drive back home so there would be room to take the gifts back. Her husband Joe was getting the time off and Alice and Bob would also drive back with them. Although everyone felt bad that the reason for getting together was because of Jack's illness, there still was a party atmosphere when they talked.

* * *

Rosie did the shopping Jack asked her to do, wrapped the gifts and then spent some time getting her home ready for Alice, Bob, and Daniel, Jack's brother. She stocked her refrigerator and was ready. She still had a business to tend to. She needed to get all the Christmas entertainment and food lined up for that. She was grateful Carl was her business partner. He worked extra so she could have the time needed to get the personal things done. They also had some wonderful people working for them who automatically filled in where needed. Rosie would have an extra generous bonus for them all.

Rosie, Sara, and Brian went to the airport to pick up the family. They stood together as the airplane landed. Sara looked at Rosie. "Do you know his family? I haven't seen a picture of them. How will we recognize them?" Both young women started to giggle, then laugh.

Brian looked back and forth at them. He didn't know why Momma and Rosie were laughing, but if they were happy, he was happy.

"I guess we look for a group that has an older couple, a younger couple with two young girls, and a college boy. If they look anything like Jack, we'll just grab them," Rose said, and the two started to laugh again and walked toward the gate.

Kindred souls they must have been, for both groups seemed to recognize each other immediately. They hugged each other, grateful that they could be there.

Little Brian took an instant shine to Daniel, who picked him up and swung him in the air.

"Me too, Uncle Daniel, swing me too," Katie and Mira begged in unison.

"Little ladies. May I remind you we are in a public place? Daniel, I think we better tone it down a bit." Grandpa Bob had spoken.

"Sorry Dad. We all needed to let off some steam after sitting so long." With a wink, Daniel set Brian back on the floor.

They went to retrieve their luggage, and Joe rented a van. It was agreed that everyone was going to the hospital and sneak in to see Jack. Sara was wondering how they were going to manage that without getting kicked out. Knowing Jack's family, they would manage a way.

Rosie walked in with Alice, Bob, and Daniel. Sara waited about two minutes and Deb, Joe, the girls, she and Brian followed. Sara held her breath as they walked past the nurses' station. She let out a sigh of relief when no one challenged their presence.

Jack was being smothered in parental love. Rosie stood to one side, letting the parents assess Jack's health. They were soon replaced with the rest of the family. In no time flat, both nieces were on the bed asking questions. Deb was busy checking if Jack was being fed properly. His mother held his hand. Jack just lay there, immersed in his family and friend's love. Actually, his friends were like family to him.

Little Brian sidled over to Daniel, reached up and took his hand.

"Hey, little buddy," Daniel bent down, picked Brian up and placed him on his hip. "Hard to see what's going on from down there isn't it?"

Sara was amazed that Brian would do that. Even at the airport he had gone to Daniel. He always hung back from strangers and stayed next to her. Maybe this family had a magic power of friendship.

The squeaking of shoes on the floor stopped all the voices. The strict, grumpy nurse and Dr. Benson came into the room and as they walked toward the bed, looked at everyone there. What happened to the 'two visitors at a time' rule?

"Dr. Benson, I want you to meet my folks and family. They just flew in from Wisconsin."

"So, you are the wonderful doctor who saved my son's life." Bob stepped around the bed, followed by Alice and reached out to shake the doctor's hand.

"And you must be that special nurse that took such good care of him," Alice added, touching the nurse's arm.

Both professionals forgot the 'two to the room' rule as they were drawn into the O'Ryan family circle and were soon busy answering questions.

If Jack's recovery progressed as it had been, Dr. Benson would release Jack in two days. It depended on the x-ray and how the lungs sounded. As the doctor looked at the family, he knew the young man would get excellent care at home.

The nurse reassessed her ideas of the two ladies. Evidently the young man came from a good Christian family, and these two young ladies were friends and there wasn't any hanky panky going on. Well at least, his mother was on the scene. She seemed like a lady. Nevertheless, she still sniffed and followed the doctor out of the room.

Rosie closed the door behind the two and started to laugh. Then she mimicked the nurse's walk and sniffed as she looked over the family. "She has never liked us from the beginning. I don't know what her problem is." Rose explained. "I keep waiting for her to ask if we were here because we're in his will!" They all laughed with her.

Alice took her son's hand. "Dad and I were very worried. I feel much better seeing you for myself. I'm told you had a couple of serious ill days. Evidently you caught a double something. But, we are here now and once we get you over to Sara's place, I am going to fix up some nice hot chicken soup and get you all well. Penicillin can only do so much. You need my chicken soup."

"Shush Mom. You go talking too loud like that around here and someone is bound to ask you for your medical license," Jack whispered loudly, then went into a coughing spell.

"Oh Jack, I think we're tiring you out. Time we all go get settled in at Sara's and Rosie's so we take turns being with you," Alice stated in a mother's voice of authority.

"That sounds like a good idea Mom, but I'll stay with Jack right now. Who knows, maybe a cute nurse will come in while I'm here." Daniel knew his parents and the girls were tired but they wouldn't want to leave Jack alone.

Bob voiced his opinion. "I agree with Daniel. I think we should go get settled in, and I bet Rosie could find us a nice cup of tea." He smiled over at Rosie.

Brian went and stood next to Daniel. The rest said their good-byes and headed for the door.

"Come on. Brian. We need to show everyone where they are staying." Sara spoke softly to her son.

Little Brian shook his head and reached up and grabbed Daniel's hand. "I want to stay with Uncle Daniel."

"Honey, Daniel is Katie and Mira's uncle. Daniel is your friend. Come now, you need to show them your books and other things so they will feel happy in our home." She reached for his little hand.

"Hey, little fella, you can call me Uncle Daniel. That's okay with me." Daniel picked up the young lad. "But you know Brian; your Mom needs you right now. You have to help everyone find their rooms and unpack. So, you go along like a big boy and I will come over later and we can throw a ball around. Okay?" Daniel handed Brian over to Sara and Brian didn't protest at all.

It was clear to Sara, for some reason, Brian had found his first hero, and it was Daniel.

CHAPTER 15

No one will ever know if it was the modern medications or the wonderful magic of family being there, but Jack got better in leaps in bounds and the doctor said he could be discharged from the hospital. Jack would need at least a week to recuperate at home and the doctor would need to see him before Jack could drive. Those were company rules.

Bob, Daniel and Joe brought Jack to Sara's place. For the umpteenth time, Alice, Deb, Sara and the children were checking to see that everything was ready. The den would be Jack's room. No stairs to climb and he could still be in the midst of everything.

"Brian, what is your favorite teddy bear doing on Jack's bed?" Sara quizzed her son.

"Teddy is always there for me and if Jack gets frightened at night, he can hold Teddy."

Alice knelt down by the little boy and put her arm around him. "Jack had a special bear just like Teddy when he was your age. I think this is so wonderful of you to share Teddy with him. But you know that bed isn't very big for Jack and Teddy. I have a feeling that Jack may want you to keep Teddy in your bed, but if he needs Teddy to hold, he will call you. Then the two of you can share Teddy." She hugged the precious child and placed a kiss on top of his head. What a lovely child. She looked up at Sara. Alice didn't have to say anything.

Sara knew how she felt. She had a lump in her throat too.

The sound of the van pulling onto the driveway sent the women scurrying to the door. Jack walked ever so slowly to the house, leaning on his Dad's arm. The other men following close behind with his small bag and medicine. The women held the door opened and everyone greeted Jack. They ushered him to the big rocking recliner. Jack sat down, exhausted from getting dressed and the short trip to the house.

"Jack Honey. Your room is ready. Would you like to get into a pair of pajamas and rest now or sit here a bit longer?" Alice touched her son's shoulder in a loving gesture.

"Mom, what pajamas? I don't own any pajamas."

"Well, young man, you do now. Dad and I went out and got you a couple of pair. Those nice flannel sweat pants type. They should be very comfortable. You are going to be in and out of bed and you aren't running around in your underwear. Obviously you haven't noticed there are ladies present. Now, I repeat, do you want to go to bed or stay here awhile?"

"Dr. Mom. Is it okay if I sit here for about five minutes, maybe get a glass of water and see where I am at?" Jack smiled at his mother.

"Five minutes. No more, then it's off to bed with you. I don't want any relapses. Later we will have the chicken soup I made for lunch. I put lots of spices in it, my medicinal elixir. If you feel up to it, you can eat at the table with us. But, young man, I will not let you over do it. Understand?" Alice was calling the shots today.

"Yah Vold, mine Dr. Mom". Jack smiled at his mother. He knew she loved him dearly.

"Here is your glass of water Uncle Jack. Sara cut up some lemon and put this slice in it. Sure looks pretty." Katie handed the glass to Jack. "Grandma said you have to drink lots and lots of water so you don't get..." her voice trailed off.

"Dehydrated." Alice added the missing word for her young granddaughter.

"I see we have a nurse to assist Dr. Mom." Jack tipped the glass like a toast to his young niece and took a large swallow of water. "Um, that sure tasted good Katie. Thank you so much getting this for me. Now I won't get dehydrated." He leaned his head back against the chair with a sigh.

"You know Mom, I think you're right. I do need to lay down for awhile."

Alice nodded her head in agreement. She was a mother, she knew about these things. Bob walked with Jack to the study. Daniel went in to help Jack get into his pajamas.

When the two men returned to the living room, Alice tipped toed in to see that Jack was okay. He was already sound asleep. She said a silent prayer for him and quietly walked out of the room. Alice had never seen her son weak like this. With his good health habits, he usually shook off any illness. A day or so of sniffles was the max for him.

Sara approached the family. "Since Christmas is just two days away, I was wondering if you all wanted to go get a tree this afternoon. I didn't buy one earlier, thinking it would be fun to pick one out together. Rosie said she would come over this afternoon and stay with Jack if we all wanted to go." Sara held her breath waiting for an answer.

Deb was the first to speak. "That's a marvelous idea Sara. We would love that! Do you have enough decorations?"

"I found the professor's Christmas things in the storage room. I bought what I decorated the house with, but I don't think he would mind if we used the decorations for the tree." Sara explained.

"We could always string popcorn and cranberries and the children could make paper chains." Bob chimed in.

"Oh Grandpa. That sounds like fun. Can we Mom, please." Katie said and joined her sister jumping up and down.

Brian just kept looking from one girl to the other. Then he joined the girls in jumping up and down. This was fun!

The adults looked at each other and nodded. It would be an old fashion Christmas tree.

Rosie told them where some tree lots were located. Sara had been in town long enough to know how to get there.

Everyone climbed into the van and they were off on a quest for the perfect tree.

"I want a big, big tree that touches the ceiling." Mira stated, "So there is lots and lots of room for Santa's presents."

"But Mira, think how many cranberries and paper chains we will have to make. I think we should only get one as tall as Daddy." Katie looked at her Dad who was driving the van. She didn't have any concept on how many strings of popcorn and cranberries it would take for a tree that size or she would have opted for one the size of Brian.

"Well, now we have figured out the height, what type of tree should we get Mom?" Joe inquired of his mother-in-law.

Laughing, Alice answered, "At this late date to get a tree, I think the question should be 'will we find any that has needles left on it'."

"Trees Momma, I see lots of trees." Brian had his nose pressed against the window looking at the tree lot as Joe brought the van to a stop. He was one excited boy.

They quickly exited the van. The girls ran ahead and were running through the few trees left. Brian pulled his hand away from his mom. He wanted to run and join the girls.

"Brian, stay here by Mommy." Sara said.

Bob put his hand gently on Sara's shoulder. "Let the boy go Sara. It's part of the fun. We're all here to watch him. He'll be safe."

Sara relented. "Okay, Brian, but stay with the girls." Sara said with a smile. Maybe she was too protective of Brian. Brian sprinted off as fast as his little legs could go.

The adults looked over the trees and it was obvious, the best ones had been taken long ago. They debated over checking other lots.

"We can go look Mother, but I think we'll run into the same situation, so I vote for staying here and deciding on one of these trees." Bob suggested.

"How about this cute little tree?" Joe stood next to a short needle tree that was as tall as he was. "I think Katie said her choice was my height."

Laughing, they all walked around the tree, giving it their pros and cons.

"The tree looks nice except for this one side, Dad. Sort of bare here." Deb pointed out the obvious to everyone.

"You know, God made all of us different, just as this tree is different. Sometimes the beauty is hidden or as we perceive it. Now, I think we can put this side to the corner and the tree will still be beautiful." Bob spoke quietly.

Alice linked her arm through her husband's and leaned her head on his shoulder. He was such a good man.

"All in favor say 'Aye'," Joe said. There was a resounding chorus of 'Ayes'. "Any Nays? No? Then, I declare this tree is ours."

Sara stood back watching the O'Ryan family. This was what she has missed as she grew up. She couldn't even remember having a tree with her birth parents. Her foster parents were good to her, but she always felt like an outsider looking in. She never wanted that for her Brian.

Brian. He was right there in the mist of things and loving every minute of this new adventure.

Joe and Bob each picked up an end of the tree to take it to the van. Little Brian quickly ran and held onto a branch. He looked back at his mom. He was so full of pride at being one of the *men*.

There was a flurry of activity as they brought the tree into the house. They finally decided to position the tree in a nice corner away from the fireplace and the men anchored the tree securely in the stand.

Sara and Deb brought out the decorations and set them next to the tree. Then Sara brought out construction paper, scissors, glue and a bowl of cranberries, needles and thread. The children got busy making paper chains.

Alice went to the kitchen to pop some popcorn to string. Bob followed her out to help.

"Bob, if you quit eating the popcorn, there might be some for the kids to string." Alice laughed.

"I only took a handful or three." Bob smiled back at her. "Besides, I'm getting hungry, my dear wife. When do we eat?"

"The soup has been simmering and is ready to eat anytime. This kitchen table is big enough to seat all of us, why don't we eat in here and not mess up the dining room. Sara has it decorated so Christmassy." Alice looked over at her husband, catching him dipping into the bowl of popcorn again.

Caught, Bob looked guiltily at her and nodded. "I think I'll go see if Jack is awake and wants to join us."

Alice shooed him away with her hand. Bob went through the swinging kitchen door with the bowl of popcorn in his hand. He would hand it over to the kids to string and then go check on Jack.

But Jack was sitting in the recliner watching all the activity; fingers getting poked as the cranberries were getting strung or full of glue as the paper chain got bigger.

Deb looked up as her dad entered the room carrying the now half bowl of popcorn.

"Does Mom need any help in the kitchen?" she asked.

"She said everything is ready to eat." Bob smiled at her. "Sara, If it's all right with you, Alice thought we could eat in the kitchen and not mess up the pretty table in the dining room." Bob looked over at her.

Sara quickly got up with a smile. "No problem at all Mr. O'Ryan. I'll go help."

"I thought we settled that 'Mr. O'Ryan' bit. I'm Bob." he smiled at her.

Sara bobbed her head yes and scooted for the kitchen.

After dinner, Daniel lit the fireplace and they decorated the tree with the unique homemade ornaments. They debated on rather or not to add any of the other decorations and finally decided to put the angel up on the top and add one string of small lights. The white skirting was put under the tree and the nativity set on the window seat, close to the tree.

Alice brought in cups of hot chocolate with lots of marshmallows in it.

"Daddy, will you read us a story now?" Mira crawled into Joe's lap and handed him a Christmas book

"Just one story young lady and then I think it's time for bed. It's been a long day." Joe hugged his young daughter.

Katie snuggled between her grandma and mother on the couch. Bob had settled into the big beige easy chair. Jack sat in the comfortable recliner. Rosie and Sara had just put away the mess made from decorating the tree, and were sitting crossed legged on some big pillows. Daniel was lying on the rug watching the fireplace, Brian next to him.

Joe began to read the story about **Frosty The Snowman**, with lots of animation. They all sang the songs with gusto. The children loved it. Too soon the story was over.

"Dad, I think it's time to get some tired youngsters to bed. Would you please give us some thoughts and a prayer to end the day?" Deb asked her dad.

Bob nodded and stood up.

Daniel sat up Indian style. Everyone else gave Bob their attention.

"This has been a wonderful day. Sara has gone to great lengths to make us all feel at home, and she succeeded. We thank you."

Sara ducked her head in embarrassment at the compliment.

"And Rosie, for your concern and hospitality, we thank you equally."

"Let us pray. 'All Mighty Father, we thank you for this day, for the fellowship, and for this special time of the year as we remember the gift of your Son, Jesus. Now, as we end this day, we ask that you bless each and everyone, heal Jack and watch over us as we travel for our night's rest. We pray this in the name of Jesus. Amen'."

And everyone responded, "Amen."

Brian had plunked down on Daniel's lap. "Will you be my Daddy and read to me?"

There was total silence except for the crackling of the fireplace. Everyone stopped what they were doing.

Sara froze. She knew she should step in and stop Brian. She didn't want him to feel rejected by his impossible request.

Putting his arms around the young lad Daniel gave him a hug. "Brian, you're such a wonderful boy, I would have no trouble being your Dad. But we have a small problem. I'm not married to your Mom and I live in another state. What if I remain Uncle Daniel for now? Uncles can read good stories too you know. Tomorrow night is Christmas Eve, and we will have a special story then."

Content with that answer, Brian nodded and put his arms around Daniel's neck and hugged him

Tears were in everyone's eyes. Sara expelled the breath she had been holding.

"Brian, it's time to get ready for bed now." Sara gently called her son.

Brian walked over to his mom. "Daniel said he can't be my daddy 'cause he lives in a different state. But he can still read a story to me, and be my uncle. I'm tired, Mommy." He let out a big yawn.

Sara smiled a look of gratitude at Daniel and reached for her son's hand.

"Off to bed now, I think Teddy is tired too," Sara said as they left the room.

"Come on girls, beddy-bye time for you two. It has been a long day." Deb stood up.

Alice turned to Rosie, "I'm going to carry these things out to the kitchen and put them in the dishwasher for Sara. Bob, help Jack to bed and then we can all leave together."

Rosie helped collect the mugs.

Jack, Bob and Daniel headed for the study.

"Dad, I want to thank you for the prayer tonight. I'm feeling much stronger. It was like a warm touch started at the top of my head and flowed through my body. I know God has blessed me with a fast healing."

Tears gently flowed down Bob's face. The three men embraced.

CHAPTER 16

Christmas Eve and the smells that permeated the house had everyone ready for dinner. There was a nice fire flickering in the fireplace and the twinkling tree lights were on. Everyone was waiting for Rosie and Daniel to get there. Daniel had spent the day helping Rosie with the final touches for the Christmas Day dinner and festivities planned for the truckers that would be at the truck plaza tomorrow.

The three young children ran and pressed their noses to the window every time a vehicle turned the corner by the house.

Little Brian was in his glory. This was all a new experience for him: a holiday to share with other kids and so many different things to do.

Finally, the long awaited car pulled into the driveway.

"Grandma. Uncle Daniel and Rosie are here!" All three children yelled out as they ran to the kitchen.

"Slow down. No running in the house." Alice bent and put her arms around the three excited children. "Let's go greet them." And holding hands, they joined the rest of the family by the door.

Through the door the sounds of one strong baritone joined by a feminine voice could be heard singing, *"Jingle Bells, Jingle Bells"*.

Sara opened the door and ushered in the singers as the family inside joined in singing the happy song.

"Um, what smells so delicious?" Daniel was sniffing the air. He handed Jack his guitar case, and started to take off his coat.

"I agree and I'm starving," joined in Rosie as she handed over a bag full of brightly wrapped gifts to Joe.

The young children swarmed around Joe as he set the packages under the tree.

"I see my name on that one!" Katie touched the gift. "And there's one with your name on it Mira."

"Do I have one?" Brian looked at Katie. His big eyes full of curiosity.

Moving all the packages around, Katie found one with Brian's name on it and picked it up. A square box wrapped in Santa paper. Brian's face was all smiles as he reached for it.

"Ah, ah, ah," Joe burst his little bubble of happiness, "You have to wait until tomorrow to open presents Brian." He turned to Alice, "Grandma? Is everything ready so we can eat, and save the presents from an early unwrapping?"

"Yes, we were just waiting for our two singers to get here. To the dining room everyone." Alice gestured with her arm.

They all stood behind a chair as they gathered around the large beautifully set table.

Sara looked at Bob. "Would you please offer the blessing?"

Bob smiled and nodded at her. "Shall we all hold hands?" He looked over this family with bowed heads and raising his head toward the heavens, closed his eyes. "Father, as we meet to partake of this bounteous food, we thank you. We thank you for each and everyone here, for your son, Jesus, the reason for our celebration. Now we ask you to bless this meal, to keep us strong and healthy and ever mindful of your presence. We ask this in Thy son's name, Jesus. Amen."

The echo of 'Amen' went around the table.

The ladies all carried in dishes from the kitchen as the men and children sat down. What a feast. Ham, potatoes, cranberry sauce, cornbread, coleslaw, raw veggies, and Deb made sure there was homemade apple pie with vanilla ice-cream later for dessert.

"Ladies, you have outdone yourselves tonight," Joe said with his mouth full of food. The others all murmured and nodded their heads.

Alice and the young ladies looked at each other and smiled. They had fun working together in the kitchen, except for Rosie who had been busy at her truck stop.

"I think I should give you all jobs as cooks." Rosie contributed to the praise of their wonderful meal. "And Sara, everything looks so beautiful. You really have a talent for decorating."

Sara blushed at the praise, but she felt so happy. "Thank you."

"Mom, I need some more mashed potatoes down here." Jack said to his mother.

Sara was glad to get everyone's attention away from her.

"I swear that boy will turn into a potato one of these days. Maybe we should have had the doctor put potatoes in your IV when you were in the hospital Jack." Alice teased her son as she handed the bowl of potatoes to him.

"Mom, don't you want me to get all well with your wonderful cooking?" Jack put a couple of spoons of the creamy mashed potatoes on his plate and looked for the gravy.

Brian looked at Sara. "Mommy, is potatoes medicine?" He wasn't so sure he was going to eat his.

Everyone started to laugh and Katie explained to Brian, "Uncle Jack loves mashed potatoes so much Brian, if we don't take our serving first, he would eat the *whole* bowl by himself. Then he would look like Santa Claus with a big belly."

Brian could understand that, and he began to eat again. But he looked over at Jack between bites and pondered of him with a long white beard. *Un, un. Jack could never be Santa Claus.*

The meal over, everyone sat around the table, drinking hot apple cider and talking about past Christmas's. There was a lot of laughter as stories of Christmas trees falling down to a live baby in the Christmas Pageant manger that didn't want to be there.

The young ones left the table to go check out the presents again. Everyone else helped clear the table and put away the leftovers. Clean up done, everyone gathered in the living room.

Rosie stood to one side of the tree and got everyone's attention." I want to thank you for letting me join in this family gathering, I feel like I'm part of it. This Christmas Eve dinner has been so nice. I know you usually have a Christmas Day dinner, but since you all will be helping me, you changed your plans. You have no idea what this means to me."

"Tomorrow will be special for all the truckers at our place and other travelers that couldn't make it home in time for Christmas. Daniel has been a great help with setting up our music area today. Sara plays the piano beautifully. We brought Jack his guitar", she looked over at him, " and if you feel up to it tomorrow, we would like you to play. Sara will be wearing a Mrs. Santa outfit and Brian will be a little elf tomorrow. Out in the car, I have two long pretty red velvet dresses for the girls and Santa hats for the rest of you, if you would like to wear them."

Sara didn't have to worry. The girls were jumping up and down, they loved to dress up.

"I'll bring them in Rosie," Daniel said and headed for the door, trailed by two happy girls.

After the girls had put on their finery and modeled for everyone, they all discussed how each one would be participating the next day.

"Uncle Daniel, you said you would read me a story tonight." Brian was getting sleepy.

"And so I shall Brian. Hey everyone. Brian wants his story."

Everyone found a place to sit. The big cushion pillows were a favorite for the young ones, all except Brian. This was his night and he got comfortable on Daniel's lap.

Putting his arms gently around Brian, Daniel began. "Long, long ago, before Grandpa Bob was born, a man called

Caesar Augustus said all his empire should be taxed. He was like the President or Governor. Everyone had to go to their own city to be taxed. In this story, Joseph and Mary had to go to Bethlehem. Now Mary was going to have a baby. She rode the long trip on the back of a donkey."

"A donkey? Why didn't they take the car?" Little Brian asked.

Mira and Katie started to laugh. "They didn't have cars then Brian." Katie said. Both girls knew this story.

"That's correct Katie," Daniel smiled. "They didn't have cars, and they didn't have huge motels like we do today. They only had small inns. When the couple got to Bethlehem, all the rooms were taken. One innkeeper said they could sleep on some straw in the barn."

Brian's eyes got real big. "With big cows and horses? I would have been afraid."

"Yes Brian. And Mary gave birth there instead of the big hospitals we have today. She had a baby boy, and they called him Jesus. They used the manger the cows ate from for his bed. Jesus didn't have a nice crib that most babies sleep in. And when this special baby was born, angels started to sing and went tell the shepherds the news, praising God, saying, *'Glory to God in the highest, and on earth, peace, and good will toward men'*."

"Why?" Asked Brian.

Mira spoke up quietly, "Because Zacharias, filled with the Holy Ghost, prophesied the birth of Jesus, the gift from God, and now he was born. We talked about it in Sunday School too."

Daniel continued, "The shepherds told everyone, they didn't have phones or televisions to do that, and three wise men from the East saw the star that had shown when Jesus was born, and came with some presents. They were expensive treasures: gold, frankincense and myrrh."

Brian sat up straight. "Those are funny gifts for a boy. I want a truck."

Everyone chuckled.

"Oh but these were very wonderful gifts Brian." Alice interjected. "*Gold* is money. Money buys food, a place to live and transportation. *Frankincense* was burned for religious rites and in embalming. The *Myrrh* is a reddish, brown healing medicine. It tastes real yucky, but very valuable. Frankincense and myrrh came from eastern Africa and Arabia. The three wise men rode their camels a long distance to bring these special gifts to the baby Jesus."

"And the birth of that baby so many, many years ago is why we celebrate Christmas. God gave us his son Jesus, our Savior. And we give people gifts that we love."

"Sara? Do you know '*Away In The Manager*'?" Deb asked.

"Yes, I do."

"Would you please play and we can sing along?" Deb requested.

Everyone agreed and gathered around the piano and sang the lovely song.

"One more request before we tuck some tired ones into bed. Jack, will you play '*Silent Night*' on the guitar?" Bob looked over at Jack.

"Love to Dad. Will you accompany me Sara?" Jack was opening his case. He came and stood by the piano.

Anyone walking past the house would have thought angels were singing inside. The melody of the voices, from the deep bass of Daniel, to the soprano of Sara was touching.

When the song ended, Jack spoke. "Dad, I would like to offer tonight's prayer."

Everyone joined hands and bowed their heads.

"Lord, I want to thank you for the gift of your son Jesus, for your bounteous love that radiates from this family and our dear friends, we consider family. I thank you for my speedy recovering. Tomorrow, as we gather to share your love with others, may your love shine out from us. In Thy son's name, Jesus, Amen."

CHAPTER 17

Christmas Morning! Katie jumped up and down on the bed and shook Mira's arm. "Mira, wake up sleepy head. Let's go see what Santa brought us!"

Mira's eyes flew open in a flash. Both girls jumped out of bed and went to the stairway. They could see the tree from where they stood, nestled in its place of honor. The small set of lights were twinkling, welcoming them to come. Leaning on the railing, they slowly crept down the curved stairs.

"Maybe we should go wake Momma and Daddy first." Mira said in a hushed tone.

"No. Let's go check under the tree and see how many presents are there." Katie reached behind her and took Mira's hand. Both girls stopped in front of the tree.

"Oh look at all the presents." Mira knelt down to touch one.

"Hey, what's this? Santa's Elves still here?" Uncle Jack ran his hand through his hair as he leaned against the door frame watching his nieces.

Startled, the girls ran over to Jack and pulled him toward the tree.

"Uncle Jack, did you ever see so many presents in all your life? We must have been *really, really* good." Katie's voice was excited. Mira bobbed her head up and down in agreement.

"Slow down girls and lower your voices. It's only..." Jack glanced at the grandfather clock. "6:00 am. I think we better go to the kitchen and make some hot chocolate and be quiet for awhile. We don't want to wake little Brian too early. It's gonna be a long day for the little fella. Plus, we aren't going to open any presents until Grandma, Grandpa, Rosie and Daniel get here, remember?"

The girls gave him a crest fallen look, but followed him into the cheery kitchen and climbed on a counter stool. Jack put the teakettle on. The girls may like hot chocolate, but he wanted some tea. On second thought, he would make a tea pot full. The house was a little chilly and everyone would like something warm when they came downstairs.

The three chatted and guessed about what was concealed in all the gaily wrapped packages. At 6:30, Jack suggested that the girls go upstairs, make their beds and get dressed. He would put on some Christmas music to gently wake the rest of the family.

The girls giggled as they ran up the stairs, thinking they were being so quiet.

Jack figured all the adults should be stirring by now. His folks had mentioned coming over about seven am so the children could open their presents, eat breakfast and have some free time to enjoy their gifts before they all headed to the truck stop to help Rosie put on a small program.

He put in some nice Christmas CD's and lit the fireplace. Going back to the kitchen he put the tea pot in a cozy, placed it, cups, some hot chocolate on a tray and carried that to the living room. Then he too got dressed and made his bed. He was feeling almost normal, not so exhausted.

As Jack came out of the study, little Brian came barreling down the stairs as fast as his little legs could carry him, his eyes glued to the tree and the array of presents underneath it.

"Momma! Hurry up! Santa Claus has been here!" His young loud voice would have woken up anyone remaining asleep. He quickly bent and picked up the box they said was his the night before and tore off the paper.

The girls flew down the stairs and joined Brian by the tree. "No Brian, you have to wait for grandma and grandpa to come."

The adults with smiles on their faces joined the group.

"Brian, stop." Sara put her arms around her son. "We need to wait for everyone so they can see the present and we can thank whoever gave it to us."

He was confused. "But you said we could open our presents Christmas morning."

"I know honey, but it won't be long now." Sara kissed her son and took the box and put it back under the tree.

"Tea. Do I smell nice, warm, hot tea?" Deb headed for the tray.

"Chocolate, nice, warm, chocolate. That's the smell." Joe sniffed the air and followed her.

"Uncle Jack made it." Mira said, skipping over to her mother. "When are grandma and grandpa getting here so we can open the gifts?"

"Right now, Mira. They just pulled into the driveway." Sara stood at the door, ready to open it and let them in.

"Merry Christmas everyone!" Bob exclaimed as he gave Sara a hug and everyone started to hug each other.

"HO, HO, HO!" boomed Daniel. "Looks like Santa was here last night!"

Brian grabbed Daniel's hand, pulling him to the pile of gifts under the tree. "Is my name on any of these? I've been a real good boy. Momma said so." Brian looked up at Daniel.

Daniel crouched down, "Yep, I see your name on one right there."

"And I have one right here." Rosie had a big bag of gifts and Alice followed with another box. Rosie not only did shopping for Jack while he was ill, she had done some of her own.

Everyone picked a warm drink of their choice and found a place to sit. Mira, Katie and Brian passed out all the gifts. They took turns opening them so everyone could see what was received and from whom. Oohs, ahs and oh look! Just want I wanted, soon filled the air. All too soon, there was a pile of torn Christmas paper, pretty ribbon and boxes strewn across the living room carpet.

The children played while the women went to the kitchen to prepare breakfast. They diced some leftover ham, added peppers, onions and eggs for a wonderful omelet. Sara squeezed fresh orange juice and Deb whipped up a new batch of cornbread.

The children didn't want to leave the toys long enough to eat. Deb and Sara said they could bring one toy to sit by them while they ate. Good conversation prevailed during the meal as they once more went over the program they would give at noon.

To soon, it was time to leave for Rosie's place. They had dressed in their Christmas clothes before they came downstairs. Rosie had done a great job of finding outfits in the right sizes. Rosie would video tape the program. They agreed the children could take a toy or two since the area they would perform in was decorated like an old fashion living room, complete with a tree, rocker and of course they would provide the people and toys.

They left in three cars. The children would be brought back later, the adults could stay and help as long as they wanted, and Rosie had her own vehicle. They sang Christmas carols on the short trip to the truck stop. Finding a place to park, they all trooped in and got ready to perform. Jack tuned his guitar to perfection, and the rest went over the music and some comedy routines they would do.

Already, truckers and other travelers were coming in for a meal, not realizing what a treat they would receive. Rosie had small little Christmas socks made up with gifts for everyone that came in. Everyone should have a gift on Christmas. The girls and Brian would hand those out. Some chairs were set up for people to sit and join in with the singing when they were finished eating.

Standing on the stage, the extended O'Ryan family looked like a Christmas card. Sara dressed as Mrs. Santa, Brian like an elf, the girls in long fancy red dresses, their hair done up in ribbons, were so cute. Deb and Alice had opted for long red skirts, white blouses, and shawls. The men had on black pants, white shirts with Christmas vests and Santa hats. Very Christmassy.

The program was interspersed with a mixture of all types of music and conversation. Many a time you saw a smile and a tear as memories flooded the many people observing the entertainment.

Jack of all people knew the loneliness of being on the road, especially at holiday time and felt pleased to share with his fellow truckers. Many of the men came up and shook hands, and patted them on the back or handed the young children money.

At first, this bothered the adults, the giving of money to the children. They talked with Mira, Katie and little Brian. "What would you think of the idea of donating the money people give you to one of the local charities that helps other people that don't have a warm place to stay or enough food to eat?" The children thought that was fine. They were happy.

Rosie beckoned to Jack. Then she took him into the office. There was a phone call waiting for him.

"Jack here."

"How yah doin', Jack Boy?" The gravelly voice belonged to no other than Lou. "Been real worried about you Kid, getting sick like that. Hard to believe, you bein' the health nut in all."

"I feet just great Lou! I don't know if it was a mixture of modern medicine, my family coming out, or God's blessings, but I will be on the road after the first of the year. My boss has a load for me to pick up on the 30th. I have to deliver on January second, so I will be dodging drunk drivers for awhile there. By the way, I want to thank you for finishing my delivery for me when I was sick."

"No problem, Kid. I always did want a chance to jump into that big ole fancy black rig of yours and drive it, just to prove I know how to handle it." Lou laughed. "You keep a nice clean set of eighteen wheels there."

"I checked it over and found some dust on it Lou. But I can live with that." Jack just had to tease.

"I just called to wish you a Merry Christmas, not check on the condition of your truck Jack. I put that black beauty back where I found it, no dents, no scratches and all the gears intact."

"Merry Christmas to you to, Lou. How are things working out with little momma and the Johnson's?" Jack inquired.

"Real good Jack. I'm having a real nice time. First family I've had in many a year." Lou blew her nose. "By the way, little momma has a name. Carol. She is starting to show a little. I took her shopping and got some maternity clothes for Christmas. Made her real happy. Got to meet my son Jason too. He's a handsome man, a good man. The Johnson's raised him right. Did I tell you the Johnson's have a small bedroom I can stay in anytime I'm close by? Carol calls me every week so I know how she's doing. She wants me there when the baby is born. Now, what do yah think about that?" Lou's voice radiated her happiness.

"Sounds like you're having a really fantastic Christmas!" Jack was pleased that Lou would share her small world with him. She was a very private person.

"Now, for the biggie. I stopped smokin'. Cold turkey. Been smokin' for at least twenty-five years. It just won't be healthy for the baby when it comes, to have second hand smoke around it."

"I must have a bad connection here. I thought you just said, 'you quit smoking'! Well, congratulations Lady! I am really proud of you! You just gave yourself the best present you could: a better, longer life! You really made my day. Ye Haw!" Jack's voice had gotten louder as he expressed his joy.

"If I'd knowed you were gonna have a coronary over it, I wouldn't have told you." You could hear the proud tone in her voice though. It hadn't been easy to stop.

"Speaking of coronary, now all I have to nag you about is eating greasy gravy and gut rotting coffee you drink by the gallon. I should say you eat with a spoon it's so strong." Jack laughed.

"Well, one day at a time Sonny. Don't want to shock my system with too many changes." Lou laughed back at him. After all, it was Christmas.

Yes, it was Christmas. Jack hung up the phone. He could hear the assorted voices as many joined in with the singing. Walking to the doorway, he leaned against it and watched the scene. Hands were clapping and toes were tapping to the beat of the music. Sara lost her shyness when she was at the keyboard, and was smiling and having fun. Several truckers had brought in their instruments. They now had a drum, trumpet and trombone. Jack pushed away from the doorway, time to add his guitar to the music makers.

CHAPTER 18

It had been a good Christmas for Jack with his family coming out and feeling well again. But like all good things, this lovely time had to end. Jack had his physical with the doctor, who declared him cured and ready to work. Jack drove back to Sara's and the family.

Reluctantly, he called his dispatcher and received all the information to pick up his load. Leaving the study, he went to the kitchen where everyone was visiting over some freshly brewed tea and hot out of the oven cookies.

"Son, if your jaw was hanging any lower, you'd kick it with your foot." Alice exclaimed. "Why so glum?"

"I just talked to the dispatcher and I leave in the morning. I'm a man. I know I have to get back to work, but it has been so nice with all you this week, I don't want it to end. Get's pretty lonely on the road."

Deb put her arm around his waist, "Quit feeling sorry for yourself brother. You know trucking is in your blood. Put you in a desk job and they would have you in a straight jacket after two weeks. Everyone knows it. Sometimes I think you and that truck are a marriage."

Everyone started to laugh. That's exactly how Jack would be: bored without the challenges that he faced everyday on the highway.

"Well Big Brother, we'll be thinking of you, out there, dodging drunks over the weekend. Actually, Sara and I are going to a New Year's Eve party with Rosie and some friends. Yep, we'll be thinking of you as we dance the New Year in." Daniel surprised everyone but Alice with this little tidbit.

"Well, Little Brother, I'll be sure and call you New Year's Day, bright and early, to check on your toes to make sure Sara doesn't step on them too much." Jack was out of his slump and the teasing was going both ways.

"Matter of fact son, none of us are going back until the end of next week. Joe took an extra week of vacation, Dan doesn't have to be back to school until the end of January and mother and I are retired. We will have fond thoughts of you all week." Bob chuckled.

Jack laughed with them all. "I'm going over and check out my marriage partner now, make sure it has good tire pressure, and take my clothes and put them away. I need to purchase some healthful snacks and water. Plus, they were going to fax my papers in at Rosie's."

"Me go too Uncle Jack?" Brian asked.

When did he come into the kitchen? The kids had been playing in the other room.

"I 'member when you gave Mommy and me a ride in your great big truck when our car stopped. You had lots of food and we had a picnic in there and I slept in your bed. That was fun. 'Member when we heard the angels bowling outside?" Brian was watching Jack.

"Yeah, Brian, I remember. It was really raining pretty hard that night. Well, you can come with me if it is okay with your mom." Jack looked over at Sara who nodded at him.

"We got the okay partner, let's go. See all of you later." Jack waved.

Brian could be heard running to get his coat. This might be a future trucker in the making. Jack was surprised that Sara let Brian go with. She was very protective of him. Jack understood why. Brian was a great little boy.

The adults visited some more in the friendly kitchen after Jack and Brian left.

"I'm glad that you're all staying here for awhile. It will be so lonely after you're gone. I'll miss you all terribly. I never would have met any of you if Jack wasn't such a Warrior of the Road and stopped and helped us in the midst that down pour." Sara said quietly.

Deb laughed, "I wormed that out of him at Thanksgiving time. That's so typical of Jack. He's *always* meeting people, *always* helping people. Maybe the government should pay him to just drive and his official title would be 'Warrior of the Road'."

"Hush Deb, you're embarrassing Sara," Alice reprimanded her daughter.

"Deb's right. That would be a great job for him. I was very lucky that night it was Jack that stopped. It could have been a robber or worse." Sara gave a shudder. "You know, I had prayed that God would help me. What do I know about stalled cars. I was alone with Brian. No food or water and it was getting so cold. The rain and wind pounded against the car. I was so frightened. When Jack stopped, I looked into his eyes and saw something that gave me the gut feeling that he could be trusted. I asked God for help, he sent Jack. I want to thank you for raising such a wonderful man." Tears were welling up in her eyes.

"Thank you for those kinds words, Sara. But Jack is Jack. May he always be an instrument for God to use. His mother and I are proud of him." Bob's voice had a calming effect on Sara.

Joe stood up. "Dad, what say we go to the store and get some steaks to grill and have a nice meal to send Jack off, as the unofficial 'Warrior of the Road'?"

Deb slid off the counter stool, "Sounds great to me. We ladies will throw a salad together; and put some potatoes in the oven to bake."

***

Rosie saw Sara's car pull up next to Jack's truck. She was surprised to see Jack open the back door and help Brian out of his car seat.

Telling a waitress she would be gone a few minutes, she slipped on her jacket and walked over to the truck. As she approached, she could hear Brian talking a mile a minute. She hiked up her skirt and climbed up into the cab.

"Knock, knock. Hi Brian." She looked at Jack. "Your paper work came in on the fax this morning. Guess you're all fit as a fiddle now."

Jack stopped putting his things in order. "Well Rosie, you know how it goes. No workie, no payie."

"I'm going to miss you Jack. It has been so wonderful seeing you every day, meeting your family and all." Rose sighed.

"What about me, I can't thank you enough for everything you've done for me, from getting me to the hospital, taking care of my truck, shopping for me, getting my family here. What a friend." Jack put his arms around her and hugged her tight. "I'm going to miss you, Rosie." Then Jack leaned down and kissed her ever so gently on the lips.

Rose reached up and put her arms around him and returned the kiss. It seemed right.

Brian piped up about that time, "Uncle Daniel did that to Mommy too. He said he had to 'cause Mommy was under the toe'. I didn't see any toe by mommy. But Uncle Daniel had a piece of a plant in his hand holding it over Mommies head." The little boy looked confused.

Rosie and Jack didn't say a thing. It might be Christmas time, but spring was in the air.

CHAPTER 19

They were eating the last meal together since Jack would leave in the morning. Bob looked around the table. It was the first time he noticed how they were all sitting like couples. He and Alice, Deb and Joe with the girls on each side of them, Sara in-between Brian and a very attentive Daniel and Rosie and Jack seemed pretty cozy.

"Mommy?"

"Yes Brian." Sara answered her son, glancing at his plate.

"Uncle Jack kissed Rosie and he didn't have any toe stuff in his hand like Uncle Daniel. Why?"

The silence was deafening around the table. Sara felt her face flush. Daniel coughed and reached for his water glass. Rosie and Jack looked at one another and Deb and Joe burst out laughing.

Bob looked at Alice. She shrugged her shoulders and shook her head. The girls kept eating. This talk didn't interest them. Chocolate pudding coming up for dessert did.

Bob with a twinkle his eyes said, "Ah, Sara, I do believe young Brian asked you a very interesting question."

"Well, Dad, it was really in the Spirit of Christmas. You know Christmas carols, Santa, presents, and the mistletoe legend that you must kiss someone if they are standing under it." Daniel spoke for her.

"And Rosie and I were just checking to see if mistletoe was really necessary to keep up the Christmas Spirit." Jack volunteered.

Rose and Sara just blushed like two high school girls. Well, it was embarrassing with Brian announcing it to everyone at the table.

Deb and Joe's shoulders were shaking uncontrollably as they tried to smother another round of laughter as her two brothers spoke. Out of the mouth of babes. They looked at each other and lost it. Her little brothers were in love.

"What's so funny Mommy?" Brian asked. Now everyone started to laugh.

When the laughter died down, Bob asked, "Is there anything else mother and I should know?"

Daniel stood up and started walking up and down one side of the room as he talked. "In this short time that we have been here, I have discovered what a wonderful person Sara is and Brian....he's one special kid." He stopped and faced his parents. "I don't want to leave. I would either like to transfer to a university out here so Sara and I can get to know one another better, or have her move to Wisconsin. We feel there is a future for us, but we need time to make sure. We can't do that long distance."

"I see. And Sara, you feel the same way?" This was an unexpected announcement to Bob.

Alice wasn't so surprised. She had seen how the young people looked at each other. But she kept quiet.

Daniel had sat back down and Sara reached for his hand. "Daniel and I talked about him finishing his last year of studies in Wisconsin, then finding work out here. I don't want to be separated that long. I think it would be very hard to know one another through email and phone calls. I would like for us to be close enough to know if this is just a holiday fling or the first steps in a lasting relationship."

"Have you given any thought to moving to Wisconsin?" Alice questioned.

"It's a big step. I'm taking a couple of classes here and I have three more months of house sitting for the professor. Plus I don't know how all of this would affect Brian. There have been so many changes in his young life." Sara responded.

Deb the little matchmaker suggested, "Why doesn't Jack let Sara rent his apartment. He's never there anyway. When he is in town, he usually stays with us. It has just been a waste of his money. Sara could check out the college and universities in town. I could watch Brian at those times, and Dan and Sara could spend some time getting aquatinted, under our watchful eyes."

"Sis, good idea! Sometimes you surprise me." Daniel turned to Sara. "What do you think of Deb's idea?"

"It would give us some together time to see how we feel. Bob? Alice?" Sara looked at the two.

"Sounds okay to me." Bob answered. "Alice?"

"A fine idea. I will be delighted to have you and little Brian around. Bob and I have grown quite attached to you two." Alice smiled at Sara.

"Hello everyone. Remember me? Did anyone ask if I am letting go of my apartment?" Jack was going to give them a gentle rough time.

"Listen little brother. This is your big sister speaking. We have decided. When you are in La Crosse, you can stay with Mom and Dad or us. You're gone weeks at a time anyway. You don't need an apartment." Deb told him.

"Okay, okay, just asking. Is there anything else you want to tell me?" Jack countered.

"Why yes, Jack. It's your turn to load the dishwasher. But first, what is going on between you and Rosie? Inquiring minds want to know." Deb smiled sweetly as she asked.

"To be honest, Rosie and I don't know. This is something new for us. I like her, she is very special." Jack said this very simply.

"I admire him." Rosie volunteered. "Where this is going, we don't know. Jack is a trucker. Life and relationships are hard on truckers. I see this every day at work. If there is something there for us, it will grow, and things will work out. If not, I'll always be his friend."

"Well, mother," Bob looked at Alice, "I think everything is under control here. How about some dessert and coffee?"

CHAPTER 20

"Man, it feels good to be behind the wheel. Now Willie Nelson's song, *'On the Road Again',* has new meaning," Jack thought as he checked his mirrors. He wondered if he could ever be happy doing anything but driving. In Sacramento, Jack had picked up a load and was traveling on Interstate 80 to Reno, Nevada.

Nevada. What an interesting state. The most common nickname is the Silver State from the vast amounts of silver that once was taken from many mines. The name Nevada comes from a Spanish word meaning snow-clad. Nevada became a state in 1864 during the Civil War and was nick named the Battle Born State. He chuckled to himself. "Guess those history lessons I studied were okay after all."

Jack watched for the casino he was to deliver to. This is a town that never sleeps. Bet I could get a pretty cheap meal from all the bill boards I've seen lately. Jack speculated. He signaled and made a right turn and found the back truck entrance to the casino. Luckily there was an open dock and he backed in.

Two young men stepped up to check Jack's paper work and get the truck unloaded.

"Pretty busy place here tonight, "Jack remarked. "How's the food? I could use a good steak about now."

"Man, they got the best in town. Good prices too," the one man replied. "I even eat here when I'm off duty."

"Sounds like a pretty good recommendation to me. Where can I leave my truck while I eat?"

"Take it out front and park down by the motor homes. We have trucks scheduled about every fifteen minutes coming in here. I don't think they would be too happy waiting while you ate a good meal and tried your hand at the black-jack table," the heavy set man said with a smile.

"Oh, I'm not in the gambling market. I work too hard for my bucks. But I appreciate your help," Jack replied.

He drove to the parking area and found a spot to park. He had about two blocks to walk back. He needed the exercise anyway.

Stepping into the casino was like stepping into another world. It was one gigantic party! He stood still and checked out the surroundings. Music was pulsing away. People of all ages winning and losing money. He located the sign that pointed the way to the eating area. Of course, he had to go past the one-armed bandits to get there.

Jack had been raised not to gamble, but the urge to just try one of the machines got his attention. Holy cats! Seventy-five cents for one pull of the handle? Jack debated. He looked around. There were more expensive machines all around. He reached into his pocket and pulled out three quarters to feed the machine, wiping his hand on his pant leg, he pulled the lever. Nada. He turned to leave; I'll try it one more time. He put in three more quarters, pulled down the lever and lights started flashing. It was embarrassing with everyone looking at him. Flustered he looked for an off button. Then security showed up.

"I didn't do anything to the machine, I just pulled the handle down and the lights went on." Jack looked from one security guard to the other.

"You're all right mister; you just won some big money. We need to get your social security number and have you sign a receipt and the money is yours," said the older of the two men.

A blond woman in a conservative black cocktail dress approached them. Reaching out her hand to shake Jack's, "Congratulations young man, you just won two thousand dollars," she smiled.

Jack sat back down on the chair. "Are you sure lady? I only put in a $1.50."

"Chalk it up to beginners luck". She laughed and held out the form for Jack to sign.

Jack filled it out and she handed over the money to him, just like that.

"Can I do anything else for you, Mr. Jack O'Ryan?"

"I'm hungry and hate to eat alone. Could you join me?" Jack wondered at his boldness.

"Sorry. We aren't allowed to fraternize with patrons. We could be accused of rigging some of the games or machines. Give me a call sometime when I'm not working." She handed him a card with her name on it. She waved and disappeared into the crowd.

The whole place was crowded with people threading their way to the next game or the ATM machines for more money. None had happy looks on their faces. Jack shook his head, so easy to get caught up in this gambling addiction.

Jack headed for the food area. Instead of a steak, he would get the biggest lobster they had in the place. Tonight was on the house, so to speak, less the $1.50.

Jack stood still in the entry way. What an array of food. It was presented like an art display. Fruit and veggies of all kinds in many different shapes, salads, cheeses and chicken, fish, steak, cooked in many different ways. Seems like a crime to eat any of it.

A cute blond in a short, short waitress outfit smiled at Jack. "Would you like the buffet or look at our menu tonight?" She leaned her head slightly to one side.

If Jack could have read her mind he would have seen: "He is cute. Real cute. I wonder if his shoulders looked as broad and muscled without his shirt on?" She gave off a soft sigh.

"I'll want the menu unless you have lobster hidden among that huge display of food."

"Menu it is. I think everything but lobster is on the tables." She laughed in a cute musical way. "Will this be a table for one or are you expecting someone else?" She didn't see a wedding band on his hand, but you never knew.

Jack noticed her name badge said 'Mary'. Rather embarrassing to look at it considering where she wore it; near some ample, almost exposed anatomy. Maybe she needed a size larger outfit.

"Just me, Mary, a typical hungry stranger in town."

"Follow me." She led the way to a small table away from the buffet. "I think you will like this one. No one will trample or spill on you as they visit the food line." She handed him the menu as he sat down. "Would you like a drink from the bar before you order?"

"No thanks, I can order now. Lobster, baked potato, small tossed salad with oil/vinegar dressing and some steamed asparagus if they have it. Ice water with some lemon in it will be fine." Jack smiled up at her as he handed back the unopened menu.

Jack watched her weave through the tables and hand in his order. There wasn't a lot to the back of her uniform either.

She must have put a rush on his order because she was back in just minutes with his salad and water.

He got a clear view of her 'ample bosom' as she took the salad off the tray and leaned over to place it in front of him. He wondered if she dressed this way when she wasn't working. Sometimes it was nice to leave a little to the imagination. Jack thought about how Rosie and her waitresses dressed: conservative yet nice. Mary probably pulled in more tips dressed this way.

"Thank you, Mary. I didn't expect service this fast." Jack smiled up at her.

She smiled back. "I need to seat the couple at the door. It shouldn't be too long for the rest of the meal."

He watched her very interesting hips sway as she walked back to the entry way, and forgot about the skimpy uniform.

Mary turned around and caught Jack observing her.

Jack flushed with embarrassment from being caught staring at her, grabbed his fork and began to rapidly eat his salad.

A heavy set middle aged man with hair combed over his balding head carried a full plate of food and sat down at the table next to Jack.

"Excuse me. I see the name on your shirt matches the name of the semi I saw in the parking lot by the motor homes. Is your truck for hire?"

"I work for the company Sir; I don't set up the deliveries. My dispatcher does that. I just pick up and deliver where he schedules me." Jack took another bite of his salad. This was a weird request from a stranger. Why didn't he just look into the phone book for a trucking firm?

"Well young man, is your truck empty? I have a load of furniture I need delivered rather quickly. It's all crated and ready to go." The man sliced off another huge piece of steak and jammed it into his mouth. He pointed his fork at Jack, and talking with his mouth full, "Can you give me the name and number of your dispatcher?"

Jack took out the small note book from his shirt pocket and wrote down the name and number on a slip of paper and handed it to him.

Mary showed up with the lobster and the rest of the meal. "How was the salad?" She asked as she put the new dishes down and removed his salad plate.

"Very good. Man, this is one big lobster!" Jack pulled the warm butter closer.

"Enjoy. Call me if you need anything else." Mary left him to eat.

In the meantime, Steak Man had been busy on his cell phone to Jack's dispatcher.

Jack's cell phone rang. "Hello."

"Jack, there's a gentleman sitting by you that has a load he wants delivered to New Orleans ASAP. I see by the computer that you are unloaded at the casino. I quoted him extra and he will have funds transferred to pay in advance as soon as you get loaded and weighed. He says there is a bonus in it for you personally for a speedy delivery. I will have one of the other boys pick up the load you were scheduled for. I'll have all the paper work on your computer when you get back to the truck. Got all that?" Sam didn't waste any time.

"Sure. Sam, I'm eating right now, and I'll let you know how I am on the log book when I get back to the truck. Are you really okay about this load?" Jack wasn't sure he trusted this guy. Just a gut feeling.

"Checked it out. Finish your meal. Give me a holler when you get back to the truck." Sam hung up.

"Well, young man, when you get through eating, I will give you the address where to pick up the load. Oh by the way, my name is Marty." He shoved his beefy hand across the aisle toward Jack.

Suddenly Jack began losing his appetite. He just didn't like this man. This was unusual for Jack. He didn't know the guy, but there was something about him he didn't trust. Reluctantly he shook the man's hand. "Jack."

Without asking, Marty took the other chair at Jack's table. "Your dispatcher tells me you are an excellent driver. The furniture is antique and well-crated, but we still want it delivered safely and quickly. Now, when you get to New Orleans, no matter what time you get there, call this number. He will give you instructions on how to get out to the mansion. Now, as soon as you are done eating, you can follow me to the warehouse where the crates are and we can get you loaded. There is a weigh scale close by. When that is done, I will transfer the funds to your company and they will give you the okay." He slid the piece of paper over to Jack.

Marty had on an expensive suit and shoes, but he didn't wear them like he was comfortable in them. There was a flashy ring on his pudgy finger that didn't come out of the Cracker

Jack box. Jack was wondering if this was a hot load. He didn't deal in stolen merchandise. Hopefully Sam was checking out the man and his credentials very carefully.

Jack took a mouthful of the baked potato and slowly chewed it for time. "Like I told my dispatcher, I need to check my log and see how my hours are. I don't drive illegal for anyone. They have expensive fines for that." Jack watched Marty to see how he reacted to that statement.

"No problem young man. We don't want you doing anything illegal, or not get your rest. I'm paying rent on the warehouse space and as soon as the boxes are on your truck, that bill is paid and my job here is done. Then it's time for a little relaxation." He gestured with his thumb at the casino and smiled.

Mary came up to the table. "How was your meal? It doesn't look like you ate very much. Is anything wrong?"

Marty ogled her openly, not even trying to disguise it.

Jack had an extreme urge to deck the guy. Man, Mary was young enough to be his daughter. His second thought was to pull off the tablecloth and cover her up.

"No, everything is fine. Do you have the bill ready?" Jack said in a controlled voice.

"Put his meal on my tab, Little Lady." Marty gave her a leering look.

Mary looked at Jack and then at Marty.

"I pay my own bills thank you. My company may have me haul your freight, but I buy my own meals." Jack didn't smile as he stood up. He didn't like this guy at all.

Mary handed Jack his bill. She picked up on the tension fast. What the problem was between them was of no concern to her. She had seen the old fat man mentally undressing her. She was use to sleaze balls like this and knew how to handle them. If they got too bad, she just had security escort them out. She might have to dress like a tramp for the job, but she wasn't going to let anyone treat her like one.

Jack put one of his new $100 bills with the check. "Keep the change, Mary. Take care." Jack started walking towards the door.

"Now, don't get testy. I was just trying to be nice." Marty threw a wad of bills down on the table, and with his bulk, tried to keep up with Jack.

Jack waited outside in the desert air for the fat man.

Marty was breathing heavy and working up a sweat when he came through the door. He was relieved to see that Jack was waiting there. But then, he did know where the truck was parked.

"What was your problem back there? I was just going to pick up the tab. Business you know." Marty was trying to catch his breath.

"Like I said, I pay my own way and I treat women with respect. I saw you leering at that young waitress."

"Well kid, the facts of life is this. You get your truck loaded and out of town, my job is done. I'm going to do a little gambling, have a few drinks and get me a woman. A young, pretty gal with a great body is always nice. Money talks in this town."

Jack didn't say a thing, just turned and started walking towards his truck. He unlocked it and checked his computer. He was disappointed that Sam had faxed in the paper work and put a 'safe to deliver' on it.

Jack wasn't surprised to see Marty had parked next to the semi. He started the truck to get the air pressure up and completed his log book while he waited. Then he called his folks.

"Hi Dad, missing you all. Say, I have a load that goes to New Orleans. I just have a weird feeling about it and wondered if you could send up a few more prayers for me?"

"Well Son, you know Mother and I always do that when you're on the road. We miss you too, son. Just be safe and don't take any chances. We have the van loaded and will head out tomorrow for Wisconsin. You'll make better time than we will. Everyone is out shopping; I stayed back to rest up for the drive. I'll tell them all you called. Love you son. God bless you."

Jack took a deep breath. Now he felt better. He motioned for Marty to go ahead. Might as well pick up the load and drive a few miles while the traffic would be light and the night air cooler.

CHAPTER 21

Why the urgency that Jack phone for directions no matter what time he arrived in New Orleans and deliver the load tonight? Jack couldn't shake the feeling that they didn't want anyone in town to know he was there.

He checked his mileage and made the call. The man answering the phone said they were about a mile and a half off the road, and to take the right turn when he came to the Y intersection. A half mile more would bring him to the old mansion.

Jack crossed his fingers that they would unload the truck quickly so he could get out of there before it was totally dark. It was creepy. A thin layer of moisture lined his upper lip. *People got lost in the bayou country real easy. He didn't want to be one of them.*

Jack was uneasy about delivering this load, and now as he pulled off the main road the hairs on the back of his neck were standing up. Was it the twilight hours or the feeling of being hemmed in on the small road by the trees of silver Spanish Moss? They brushed against his truck like giant spiders trying to get into the trailer contained furnishings for an old mansion that some rich dude was restoring.

He peered around as he slowly negotiated the bumpy, narrow road, hoping this swampy area wasn't boggy. He could live without getting the truck mired. He knew there were all kinds of wild-life living out here. He preferred snakes and alligators as shoes, not visitors.

Jack's pulse started to race with the eerie feeling that he was being watched. All the stories about voodoo came to the surface. Jack shook his head. He was letting his imagination get the best of him.

He was negotiating a sharp curve when he caught something in his headlights that looked like a body lying in the middle of the road. Instantly, he hit the brakes. Thank goodness he had been driving slowly or he would have run over it. He wondered if this was some bizarre trap to steal his truck and cargo. He looked around and checked his side mirrors. Nothing was moving. Even the branches on the trees were dead still.

Taking a deep breath, Jack grabbed his six-cell flashlight for protection and, with trepidation, left the truck to see who was abandoned in this God forsaken marsh.

Jack cautiously approached the figure on the gravel road. It was a woman. She remained on her side in a crumbled heap. There had been no movement from her at all since Jack had stopped the truck.

On the alert, Jack looked around then slowly knelt down and touched her shoulder. "Hey lady, you okay?"

Her body rolled back and she let out a soft groan.

Jack inhaled sharply. Her face was all bloody, both eyes swollen shut, and her lips were split like a boxer had hit her. The bruises on her neck, up and down her arms, and her torn clothes indicated she had given her assailant quite a struggle.

Jack turned on his flashlight and saw the trail she had made to get this far. He wondered where she found the strength to crawl at all in her condition. He didn't hear or see anything out there.

He checked her pulse and jumped when she moaned out in a whisper, "Help me."

"Who did this to you?"

Her lips moved slightly but Jack couldn't hear a thing.

Glancing around once more, he leaned closer as she whispered.

"Y. River. Lights three times. Contessa." Jack repeated it out loud. He wasn't sure if this was what he heard or not. He couldn't ask her again. She had fainted.

Jack leaned back on his heels in a quandary. He didn't have much time. The men at the mansion knew he was on his way there and no doubt they were looking for him. The girl evidently didn't want anyone in that direction to know she was still alive. If they caught him with the girl, they might do him in too. He didn't have the foggiest idea why he thought that, just a gut feeling they would.

"Well God, I can't leave her on the side of the road, so I guess You had better help me out." Jack sent up the swift prayer as he gently gathered the unresponsive girl in his arms and headed for the truck. She didn't weigh much, but he struggled as he climbed up into the cab with her inert body and placed her on his bunk. He covered her up with the sheet and partially closed the curtain behind his seat.

Quickly leaving the truck, he grabbed a small branch with leaves on it and tried to brush away his footprints and her crawling marks from the road. If anyone followed her, let them think the bayou spirits got her.

Sweating profusely, he nervously got back into the truck. The thought came to him to act like a dumb hillbilly when he reached the mansion. He used some waterless cleaner on his hands and took off his bloody shirt. Pulling out a dirty wrinkled one from his bag, he jammed the discarded one in its place. Leaving a shirt tail out, he put on a baseball hat with the brim turned to the back. Turning off the air conditioner, he rolled down the windows, put the truck into gear and praying, continued down the narrow road.

As he pulled into the rounding crushed rock driveway, six guys came lumbering out of the house. The yard light cast ghostly shadows around the area. One of the men with a can of beer in his hand strolled up to the truck.

"Took you long enough to get here. Expected you 'bout ten minutes ago." The gruff voice wasn't friendly.

Jack leaned his arm and head out the window, "Y'all didn't tell me that it was a dang gum billie goat trail. Man, my trailer was a bouncing all over the place. Had ta slow down. Whee, it's a hot one. Air-conditioner done went out yesty day and the boss told me to wait till I plumb get back ta fix it, 'Nough to make me want to quit." Jack drawled this all out with a twang and spit into the dirt by the man's feet. "Whard y'all want this unloaded?"

"Back it up to that shed over there. We ah, have some work yet to finish before they want the furniture in the big house."

"Okey dokie with me. Might want to spot me a bit. I ain't none too good yet a backin' up." Jack kept up his charade. He made a big deal about getting the truck in the right gear and taking a second try to get the semi properly backed up to the shed. He slowly climbed down and sauntered back to the trailer. Sweat was trickling down from his armpits and his shirt was sticking to his back. It wasn't from the sultry weather. One of the men had a holstered hand gun attached to the back of his belt. Jack bet they each had one.

Continuing his role of a puffed-up new driver, Jack made a big show of finding the right key, and unlocking the trailer. He swung open the heavy doors and pulled down the ramp. Then he picked up the clipboard. "Sez here I have a hunnerd and fifty crates. After we get this unloaded, y'all can sign for it and we'd be done."

As Jack unhooked the dolly from the side of the trailer and proceeded to bring the crates to the end of the trailer he sent up a silent prayer that the girl wouldn't make any noise. He had a gut feeling that neither one of them would be found alive if she did.

The men pitched in to unload the truck, and it wasn't long and it was empty. Jack thought it was weird that the whole time the men worked, no one said anything.

"I need someone's John Henry on this paper." Jack held out the clipboard.

The man who seemed to be in charge grabbed it from Jack, without verifying the figures, signed the invoice, and tore off his copy. Then he thrust the clipboard back to Jack.

"Much obliged mister. Man, I'm gonna go back and get me a motel room tonight and a cold beer. Maybe two. Yes sirree bob. I ain't a sleepin' in this hare hot truck again tonight, don't care what the boss says. How do ya'll stand this heat?" Jack took off his hat and wiped his sweaty forehead on his arm.

"You get use to it, and the quarters we sleep in have air-conditioning."

"Y'all must have a dang good boss." Jack turned and headed for the cab in a forced slow nonchalant gait. He hoped no one followed him and looked inside the cab. He turned and waved as he climbed up the steps. Once again, he messed with the gears and with a jerking start headed back the way he came in. He didn't let out his breath until the lights from the yard were out of his sight. *I deserve an academy award for that performance. His truck might need a new transmission.*

Glancing back at his bunk, he saw that the young lady was in the same position. He sincerely hoped she wasn't dead. He didn't want to stop the rig and check in case he was followed.

Once out of sight, he drove much faster than he had come in. As he approached the Y in the road, he contemplated going back to town and calling the police. What was he going to tell them? Would they accuse him of beating up the young lady? He hesitated for a moment and then turned towards the river, his stomach in a knot. This would come under the heading of being between a rock and a hard place.

CHAPTER 22

Was he exchanging one danger for another?

Jack stopped the rig and flashed his lights on and off three times like she had instructed and then just left the parking lights on.

He was sweat soaked shirt stuck to him. He felt like a sitting duck.

Jack kept scanning the area around him. In the dark, humid night, he didn't see or hear the man until he stepped up to the truck. Jack jumped as the stranger spoke, surprised he didn't have a heart attack.

"You flashed your lights. Why?" The brim of the man's hat shadowed his face. Somehow Jack didn't feel threatened as he had by the men at the mansion.

"Contessa," Jack said.

The man leaped to the side of the truck, sticking his arm through the open window, grabbed the front of Jack's dirty shirt. "Where is she? Who are you?"

"Take it easy, mister. I don't know if the woman in the back is Contessa or not. I found her lying in the middle of the road when I took a delivery to the mansion. She rallied enough to tell me they tried to kill her, to help, to come here and flash my lights and say the word 'Contessa'. Then she passed out."

Jack removed the man's hand from his shirt and slid out of his seat and moved to the back.

Not asking, the stranger opened the door, climbed in, and knelt to look at the woman. Grief registered on his face when he saw how battered and bruised she was. "We take her to Granny."

Jack didn't know if the 'we' meant he had no choice, or if the man needed his help. Either way, Jack wanted to know what was going on.

Working together, they wrapped her in the blanket and got her out of the truck. She moaned softly even though they tried to be gentle.

"What about my truck?" Jack asked.

"Don't worry," the stranger replied softly. "Your truck will be safe, you have my word. It will be watched. Come."

Jack shut off the truck and slid the keys in his pocket. He peered into the darkness, but didn't see anyone else. He made a mental note to get his eyes and hearing checked if and when he got safely back home.

The other man carried Contessa to the small boat. Jack stepped in and held out his arms for the woman. The stranger took the oars and silently rowed them a short distance to what appeared in the dark to be a houseboat. Jack didn't know how the man found his way without a lantern and there definitely weren't any street signs around.

A small elderly lady stepped out onto the porch with a lantern. "Who goes there?"

"Just me, Granny. We have Contessa. She's hurt real bad," the young man said as he secured the boat to the house. He scrambled onto the deck and Jack managed to lift Contessa up to him without tipping the small craft over. Then he stepped up.

"Who this man be?" The old lady squinted at Jack.

"The one who found Contessa. You were right all along Granny. They did have her. You want me to float down to Auntie Kate's?"

"Better. May need some help with things," was her terse reply as she followed them inside.

Jack didn't know what to do or think about all of this. He stepped back outside and tucked in his shirt. He must smell to high heaven in his dirty, sweaty shirt.

Without a word, the young man came out and started to pole the houseboat.

Jack grabbed another pole, and copied what the other man was doing. Jack didn't have the foggiest idea *where* he was or *where* he was headed, or who Auntie Kate was. But he wanted to know what was going on. He thought it best to keep quiet right now.

There were many night sounds Jack couldn't identify: rustlings, calls, and grunts. Every so often he would hear a swoosh or splash and wondered what it was.

"What's the noise I just heard?" Jack asked his silent companion.

"Gators."

Jack stepped back away from the edge. Now wasn't the time to fall in.

"My name's Rafe." He paused long enough to extend his hand to Jack in a warm, but firm handshake. "Thanks for helping our Contessa."

"Jack. Pleased to meet you. Would you mind telling me what I got myself into, what's going on, and who would beat up Contessa?"

"Be patient a few more minutes. We're almost at Auntie Kate's," Rafe replied. He no more than said that and they rounded a bend in the river. There, against the bank was an identical houseboat like they were poling. Granny's houseboat scraped gently against the wood and Rafe secured the two houses together.

A huge black lady with a bright red scarf wrapped around her head and many necklaces making a soft jingling noise, stepped out on the deck. "That you Rafe boy?"

"Yes, Auntie Kate. Contessa is hurt real bad. They caught her and tried to kill her. Granny needs your help."

Auntie Kate shook her head and her gold hoop earrings swung back and forth. "I warned the chile. I saw it in the cards." The old lady murmured as she stepped over to the other house. "She should have waited for the potion. It would have protected her."

Jack got goose bumps and the air was still warm and humid.

Auntie Kate stopped in front of Jack and put her hands on her generous hips. She tipped her head to one side, her eyes raking over him from head to foot. "He not the one. He carry a good spirit."

Jack let out a sigh of relief. Up to that moment he had a feeling he could have been dinner for one of the gators, if she had so designated.

Then she turned and for a big lady, quietly went through the doorway. "What we have Granny? What they do to our honey chile?" she asked in a concerned tone.

With the murmur of the two women in the background, Rafe motioned to wooden chairs against the wall. Doctoring was woman's work. They would stay out of the way unless they were needed. The two men sat down. Rafe filled his pipe before saying anything. The air soon filled with a sweet smell of cherry.

The suspense was getting to Jack, as he took a closer look at his surroundings. There was a waist-high railing around the narrow walk along the sides with a porch in front where they were sitting. It was a small house that floated. Very different from what he was use to.

Rafe had been intently watching Jack, his brown eyes missing nothing. "Now, we talk. What was in the load you took to the mansion?"

"Furniture I was told." Then Jack related the events that had transpired until he met up with Rafe at the river.

Rafe nodded his head. He took the pipe from his mouth, "What you think, boys?" Rafe asked.

Two men came around the house on the small walk way ever so silently, like panthers in the night.

Jack didn't know where they had come from and hadn't heard a thing. Spooky. He bet his blood pressure must be in the danger area.

The taller of the two men took a chair, and straddled it facing them. "He tells the truth, Rafe. We saw the truck take the mansion road. We were looking for our Contessa, and saw him help her. At the time, we didn't know if he was one of them or not. We took the shortcut to the mansion and everything is like he said."

Jack started to sweat again even though the night air was getting cooler. He knew he had felt eyes on him, but he never saw a thing. What a relief! He wasn't going nuts after all. He was still going to have his eyes checked.

Rafe stood up and went to the door. "Granny, how is she?"

"Got the chile all cleaned up. Don't 'peer any bones broke. They 'most choked her to death. She must have faked them out. Come in. I want to see that young man, then I makes food and coffee for you." Granny stood at the entryway and opened the screen door.

All the men stood up and motioned for Jack to go first.

Jack ducked his head and entered the room. It had a mixture of herbal smells, onions, garlic, and many he couldn't recognize. The furnishings were old and well polished. The pieces of furniture looked hand crafted to fit the space. Everything was neat and clean.

Granny reached up and took his face with both hands and kissed first one cheek, then the other. "Gracés mon ami." Then she turned to the stove and started moving the pans around.

Auntie Kate was sitting in an old rocking chair next to the small cot where Contessa lay swathed in bandages. There were assorted bottles of different things around her and some type of incense burning. Auntie Kate was saying a chant, softly like a prayer.

The atmosphere in the air had changed for Jack, from suspect to friend.

Rafe pointed to the table. "Have a chair Jack, I'll get the coffee." The other men took chairs at the table.

"I'm really dirty and need to wash up. My shirt smells pretty rank too."

Rafe laughed, showing his white teeth against his light tan skin. "You're right about that. I'll show you where you can wash and get you one of my shirts. Come." Rafe took Jack into the next room which was partitioned off with colorful material. There was a small bathroom. The toilet must have gone straight into the water. There was an overhead water holder, a small sink and a stack of towels and wash clothes. A bar of homemade soap rested in an oval dish unlike anything Jack had seen before. He bet an antique dealer would give them a lot of money for it.

Rafe got Jack a clean shirt and left him to clean up.

After sponging off the grime in cold water, and hand combing his hair, Jack returned to the men in the other room.

"Your shirt fits real nice, Rafe. We're about the same size." Jack smiled. "I rinsed mine out and will change back when it's dry."

Rafe just waved his hand. "No matter."

"Now, will you enlighten me why someone would beat up Contessa. Who are all of you, and what is going on?" Jack was brimming with curiosity.

"You eat first." Granny stated as she put food on the table. The aroma made Jack's mouth water and he realized he hadn't eaten since breakfast. Fried potatoes with onions, fish of some kind with okra and the nicest fluffy biscuits. She refilled the mugs with hot coffee which the men put generous spoons of sugar into. The men started to eat. No one crossed Granny.

With his mouth full, Rafe pointed the knife he was buttering his biscuit with first at the taller man and said, "My cousins Manny and Cray. Contessa is my sister. Granny is my father's mother and raised us after our parents died. Auntie Kate has always been here."

Jack nodded to both men and glanced at Auntie Kate who was changing the poultice on Contessa's face. Auntie Kate was still praying or chanting as she worked and ignored the men.

"We have other family members watching your truck. It will be safe. You are safe. We are in your debt for saving our Contessa. We won't forget." Manny spoke up for the first time.

His hunger sated, Jack leaned back into his chair and took a sip of the strong coffee. Now he knew why they added so much sugar. "I am safe from what? I still don't know what's going on. *Why* is someone spending so much money on an old home so far in the wilderness? *Why* did those men have guns? *Why* did you let Contessa go to the mansion alone and *why* would anyone want to hurt her?"

The other men looked at one another and then over at Granny. Granny made eye contact with Auntie Kate. An unspoken agreement passed between them.

Granny pulled her smaller rocking chair up by the men. "My husband, Chase and his twin brother Clive inherited that mansion from their father. It was big enough for the whole family. Oh, we had a wonderful time living there. Chase and Clive each had a wing upstairs for our families and we all used the downstairs for entertaining." She smiled and rocked as the memories of years ago flooded her mind. "The families were to share in all things. We had many small business ventures from seafood to crops supporting us then. All the cousins worked. Parties, dances and visitors from all over kept the mansion busy. Even the governor was a frequent visitor. We were very important, very well off. Then Clive married that outsider." Granny said 'that outsider' with venom in her voice.

Auntie Kate started to mutter. "She was evil, she wanted nothing but money. She was flashy, a drinker, and didn't want any poupèe. Clive wanted an infant to carry on the family name. She didn't want to ruin her figure. They fought. She tried to break up the family. Clive made out a will leaving everything to Chase and his family if there were no infant. She devil woman."

Granny nodded in agreement. "One day after a big party, Eve left with one of the male guests she had been making eyes with. About two months later, she sends Clive a letter that she is expecting Clive's child. No return address, nothing. Seven months later we get another unsigned letter saying she died in childbirth. For some strange reason, Clive didn't believe that. He still loved her and kept searching for them, but he never found any clue as to if the story was true or where they were. He never got over this loss. Slowly he lost his will to live and died. The town doctor said it was his heart."

Auntie Kate hissed from the other side of the room. "Black magic."

Once more, Jack felt goose bumps raising the hair on his arms.

Granny continued, "My beloved Chase and I have our children and raised them in the mansion. The war came and everything changed. Then, I lose my Chase, and Rafe and Contessa lose their momma and papa in a plane accident and I close the mansion. I cannot live there anymore. It is too sad. But the will is left in the secret place in the mansion. The mansion belongs to Contessa and Rafe. But they are happy on the river."

Rafe speaks. "Then about three months ago, this man shows up, asking for Granny. He says he is Jake, the son of Clive and Eve, and wants his share of the inheritance. He wants the mansion. We say it is not his, it is ours. He says he has the will and we can't stop him. He plans on restoring the mansion and open a gambling casino. Granny tells him no one can be happy or productive there until the curse is removed. He laughs and calls us stupid, superstitious Cajun people."

"Our Contessa tried to talk with him, asked to see the will, but he just laughed. We know he doesn't have the will. Grandpère hid it in a secret place and made up a song up about it that he used to sing to us. As children, we could never figure out by the song where he put the will."

"One day Contessa said the tune mysteriously popped into her head. She's sure she knows where the will was hidden.

Hopefully, with the remodeling, which we think they were really tearing the place apart to find the real one, they haven't found it or destroyed it. We know it was wrapped in a small leather pouch."

Rafe was interrupted by Auntie Kate. "Yesterday, Contessa said she was going to sneak over and retrieve the real will. I told her to wait. I tell our Contessa the cards say it is the wrong time. I will make strong potion to protect her, to wait till the moon is not full. She not listen to Auntie Kate, she say 'not enough time Auntie Kate', and my beautiful chile slip away." Auntie Kate shook her head slowly, a sad look on her face.

Jack could see she loved the young girl like a mother.

Once more Rafe picked up the story. "We men were going to go over after we had a plan and investigate more, but she went without any of us. Evidently his hench -men found her and tried to force her into giving them the real will, but she wouldn't talk. Luckily she got away, and you found her. Now, this impostor must pay. We also think he is dealing in illegal things. But until we can retrieve the original will that is well hidden, and find proof, we can't do anything."

"Why don't you go to the law? Didn't any of the other adults know where your grandfather put the will?" Jack asked.

"The leader, which in this case, was Grandpère, took care of matters. No one questioned his actions, and he managed everything, and he didn't expect to die so early," Rafe explained.

For the first time Cray spoke up. He spoke with an educated voice. "We are the law here now. We are mostly Cajun people. The law out there doesn't concern itself with us. Even though we have lived on this land for about two hundred years, unless we can find the original paper that also has the deed on it, his forgery will probably hold up in court."

"So what are you going to do?" Jack looked at the men.

Cray answered. "We have sent word for the family to gather tomorrow. We have some here already, watching your truck and the mansion."

Auntie Kate spoke. "When our chère wakes and can talk, then you can go. Now, I go read the cards and prepare the potions for the blessings. It is time to cleanse the mansion and land. The spirits have spoken." She stepped over to her house.

Granny took the vacated rocking chair next to Contessa and began changing the dressing once more.

Jack looked around. Everyone was shaking their heads in agreement. He was totally amazed. After all these years, now they want the land to be prayed over, used and lived on. Once more be productive, alive.

Tomorrow the men would gather and plan their strategy, *after* Auntie Kate did her magic. Jack didn't see any phones. How did the word get out? Maybe with their Choctau Indian, French, African, and Christian mixture of beliefs, they tapped into a different level of communication. Jack thought he would stick to prayers and Ma Bell.

For now, the men entertained Jack with stories about how it had been at the mansion when they were children. They had been happy children.

Then without a sound, Auntie Kate returned and said to Jack, "Say good night to Contessa and Granny. You stay at my house."

Jack didn't know how such a heavy woman could walk without making a sound or motion on the house. Jack nodded. He didn't have any other options. He didn't see any motels with neon lights around. Stepping over to the cot, he looked down at Contessa and received a huge surprise. Whatever concoctions Granny and Auntie Kate had made and used on her, the swelling was almost gone from her face. He stood there not realizing he was speaking aloud. "Lord, continue to bless this girl and heal her. Be with all of us this night as we sleep. We give you thanks, Amen."

Then he turned and gave a slight bow to Granny, "Thank you for the wonderful meal. I appreciate your hospitality."

She nodded at him. She hadn't expected this outsider to pray for her grandchild or the rest of them.

"We go." Auntie Kate gently touched his arm. Jack's short prayer reinforced her opinion of him. He was a good man. The spirits had told her true.

Jack gave a short salute to the men and followed Auntie Kate. He had a longer prayer to send God. *Quietly* this time.

CHAPTER 23

Jack woke up to the pungent smell of coffee brewing. He could hear the soft scuffing sound of slippers going across the wood floor. At least Jack hoped it was slippers he was hearing, and not something that normally lived in the water. His eyes flew wide open as he remembered where he was! He sat up straight and looked around. Yes, he was still on a houseboat in some remote bayou in Louisiana. It wasn't a bad dream after all.

"Good morning my young friend. I trust you slept well." The rich low voice of Auntie Kate broke the silence.

Jack swung his legs to the side of the cot and ran his hands through his hair. He yawned and stretched his arms as he stood up. "Yes Auntie Kate, I had a good night's rest. With everything that transpired yesterday and drinking strong coffee so late in the evening, I didn't think I would sleep a wink."

Jack turned to straighten the covers on the cot when he noticed his shirt from yesterday had been laundered and ironed. He picked it up and turned around to see Auntie Kate watching him with her dark brown eyes. "When did you have time to do this? I only rinsed it out. Thank you very much." Jack wondered if she had slept at all last night.

Auntie Kate acknowledged his thank you with a nod of her head, causing her gold earrings to jingle softly. Today her head was wrapped in a silk scarf the shade of electric blue that made her dark brown eyes sparkle. She gestured toward the curtained off area. "You wash up there, food ready."

The tantalizing smell of food made Jack's stomach growl and he completed his morning ritual quickly. Stepping through the curtained doorway, he was surprised to find, Rafe, Manny, and Cray, sitting at the table with mugs of steaming hot coffee in front of them. He had not heard anyone come in. These people all moved so quietly. He was ready to put bells on their moccasins.

"Morning, gentlemen. How is Contessa today?" Jack took the empty chair.

"Ready to talk with you," Rafe replied taking a huge bite of bread.

Jack found that hard to believe. He shook his head. "She was in pretty bad shape last night," he said quietly.

Auntie Kate was suddenly by his elbow with the huge coffee pot, using her large, white apron as a potholder, poured strong coffee into his cup and refilled the other men's cups. "You eat Mr. Jack. Then we go see our Contessa. Potions and prayers make her fine. She needs much rest. Granny and I take good care of our chér." Auntie Kate said in a matter of fact tone.

The men shared glances, lowered their heads, and resumed eating. Auntie Kate had spoken.

While the men talked, she placed bowls of oatmeal topped with cinnamon, and thick slices of freshly baked bread spread thick with creamy butter, in front of the men.

"Jack, the family has gathered during the night. I don't want you to be alarmed when you see the extra boats and people around. We have plans to make. But we needed to wait until we could talk with Contessa." Cray spoke softly.

"How?" Jack choked on his mouthful of food. "How did you contact everyone? I haven't seen one phone around."

Manny just shrugged his shoulders. "The family just know when they are needed. It is the bayou way."

Jack got that prickly feeling again on the back of his neck. He would have rather heard that the men had cell phones or walkie talkies. His appetite vanished.

Finished eating, the men stood and went to the screen door. Jack was amazed. Two more house boats had joined them during the night, plus numerous small skiffs. There were about twenty men on the small porches of the four homes. The men smiled and parted to make way for Auntie Kate, Jack, Rafe, Manny and Cray to enter Granny's door.

Jack got his second shock of the morning when he entered Granny's home and saw Contessa sitting in the rocking chair getting her long jet black hair brushed by her grandmother. Gone were the swollen eyes and lips. There was a faint bruise around her neck. Her arms were covered by the long sleeves of a white nightgown, so he couldn't tell if the black and blue marks she had on them had vanished too.

He looked over at Granny and Auntie Kate and then back at Contessa. He believed in miracles, but he had never seen one like this.

Granny motioned Jack to come closer. "Contessa, Jack, the man who saved your life. Jack, my granddaughter, Contessa."

Contessa reached out her hand to Jack. "I'm most grateful to you Mr...."

Her voice was still raspy from almost being strangled to death the day before.

"O'Ryan, Jack O'Ryan. I'm amazed at the change from last night. I prayed for you, but God has more than taken the pain away, He has removed all the bruises from your face!"

"Spirits tell me what potions to use." Auntie Kate muttered from behind the chair where she stood with her arms folded across her amble bosom. *Outsiders just didn't understand our ways.*

Rafe stepped up to them. "Contessa, we have many of the family here and have plans to make. We, the men, plan on visiting the mansion today. We need to know where to find the will and deed. Do you remember the song Grandpère sang to us and what you think the interpretation of it is?"

Contessa took a sip of the concoction in her cup, and then began to sing softly in her hoarse voice.

> "Merry merry little star,
> You are so close, yet so far.
> Gone in daylight, back at night,
> Basking near the fire light."

The men looked at each other with blank expressions on their faces.

Contessa leaned her head back on the chair, her eyes were twinkling with excitement.

Manny knelt down by the arm of her chair. "Cousin, we are thankful to the powers that be for your miraculous recovery, and when you are totally on your feet, I personally plan on scolding you for getting into such a dangerous situation! For now, will you please be so kind as to explain the riddle to us?"

Contessa reached over and patted his head.

Manny reached up, took her hand and kissed it. He loved her like a sister. "Everyone is here. We are going after the will and take possession of the mansion. Time, my chèr is of the essence."

Contessa nodded her head. "Remember the great wooden doors at the front of the house? Picture yourself in the great entry hall and face the doors. What do you see? The lead windows in the upper part of the doors are vaguely shaped like a huge blurry star. The massive frame above the doors have brass studs embedded in star a shape. Now turn around and you see the huge mirror above the fireplace. When the moon would shine through the windows, the reflection bounced off the mirror to the studs on the upper door frame. The secret panel has to be there." She said leaning back against the chair back, exhausted.

"She be right. I remember now that papa had hidden panels by all the double doors. There is a small lever at the very top where you can't see it." Granny was nodding her gray head.

The murmur of voices from the men took on an excited tone. Armed with this information, they were ready to go claim the family mansion.

"Wait!" Contessa waved her hand to get the men's attention. Her soft voice wasn't heard.

"Stop!" Auntie Kate boomed out the word and the silence was deafening.

"Contessa has more to say."

"Dogs. They have four vicious ones they let loose in the mansion at night. They threatened to put me in there with them. I was so scared." She shivered.

"Not to worry. I make a sleeping potion for the dogs that will make them sleep like little puppies." Auntie Kate reassured her.

Rafe took control of the meeting. Everyone was quiet.

Jack raised his hand to speak. "Rafe, I'm worried too. I counted six men and they all had guns. No telling how many men or weapons I didn't see. You can get control of the dogs, but what is your plan to subdue the men without anyone getting shot or killed?"

Cray stood up next to Jack and Rafe. "Very simple. Remember when we told you how we played and had so much fun as young kids at the mansion? Great grandpère built the mansion and many of the buildings. At that time, many strange things could happen in the bayou. Therefore all the rooms and buildings have secret entrances and passages to escape to the water. I remember some of them. I spoke to my papà and he drew me a map." Cray pulled a folded piece of paper out of his pocket and spread it on the table.

"Here's what I suggest. Tonight the moon will be full and will give us some light. The men watching Jack's truck and the road have been instructed NOT to let anyone in or out. They will stay there. The rest of us will divide into four teams. Rafe, Manny, Frank, and myself will each lead a team."

"Frank is good with animals. He and his men will take the meat with the potion and make sure the dogs are asleep and secure them in cages. They will then take positions at all entryways of the house. Frank, you can either enter by one of the passageways or however you find best. We will give them forty-five minutes head start."

"Manny and his group will have surveyed the area for guards. So far, we haven't found that they post any. They will then surround the area and only advance when they are needed.

Rafe and men will go to the two buildings the hired men are staying at. I will take the rest of the cousins. Both groups are going to basically smoke out the workers. They have the air-conditioners on and that will mask most of our noise.
Hopefully we can get the smoke bombs lit and in the buildings at the same time." "Where do I come in with this plan?" Jack asked.

"You don't. We cannot risk you getting hurt." Cray said.

"Well, you can't, but I can. I want to help round up this band of thugs that almost killed Contessa. I will personally be happy to load them in the semi and drop them off at the police station. You didn't plan on alligator justice I hope! And who is going to watch the women while we are all gone?"

Auntie Kate reached under the bed and produced a shotgun. "I am."

Jack had no doubt of that.

"Okay, any other questions? Then we meet at seven tonight by Jack's truck. Those that will be greeting the smoked-out men have rope and duct tape to tie them up with. We want to do this peacefully without anyone getting hurt. At nine o'clock everyone will be surrounding the grounds. Frank and his group will wait until the dogs are put into the mansion and the men have all gone to their buildings. We'll give Frank his forty-five minutes to put the dogs to sleep. By then the lights should all be off. Once the last building goes dark, we wait another fifteen minutes, and then we enter and light the smoke bombs. Everyone be careful. Frank, can one of your men hit the yard lights and mansion lights once our coughing men start coming out?"

Frank nodded in the affirmative.

"Good. I have a map drawn out for each leader detailing the entry ways, and our positions. Everyone look it over carefully. Then eat, take a nap, ask the spirits of the bayou, and God to protect us. Thank you all for showing up. Until tonight, adieu."

CHAPTER 24

In the quiet night, the men waited in their positions. Frank and his group left about fifteen minutes earlier to put the dogs in la-la land. Jack checked his watch again. His nerves were starting to get to him. He was fine when they were moving into position, but just sitting here, waiting, was making him jumpy. He strained his ears for sounds of the undergrowth. Um, he supposed snakes traveled at night too,
but how far do alligators roam?

Manny poked Jack gently with his elbow and pointed to the buildings. The lights were all off. It was almost time to start the show. Manny looked at the moon, Jack at his watch. It was time.

Slightly bending to blend with the surroundings, Manny lead the way, Jack and three other men followed single file. Each carried some rope pieces and duct tape. The others were armed with knives. Jack had his tire checker. Hopefully this would be a peaceful takeover with no blood shed or bones broken.

At the edge of the bunkhouse, Manny went to the back with two men, as Jack and the other man readied themselves by the front door. They silently screwed two stakes into the ground on both sides off the entryway and attached a small wire to them. As the men stumbled out of the house, this would trip them and Jack and his cohorts, if all went as planned, would have them tussled up before they knew what happened.

Silently, the two men that had been with Manny joined them. They had fixed the back door by the kitchen so it wouldn't open. The men in the house would have to come out the front door. Now the odds were pretty even. Manny joined them and gave a thumbs up.

Peering across at the lodge, they barely saw the small pin light flash three times. Rafe and his group were ready too. Now let the smoke bombs do their job.

Soon Jack could smell the acrid smoke. He wondered how much longer before the men inside reacted. He didn't have long to wait.

"Wake up! The house is on fire! Where's the damn light switch? Everyone get up."

Jack could hear the men responding to the call. There was panic going on inside. Just as the door of the bunkhouse burst open, so did the door from the lodge.

The men were coughing and bumbling around.

The first man out of the bunkhouse tripped over the wire and went down with a thud. Two of the men with Jack grabbed him and tied him up fast. The next one came out trying to wipe his eyes to see; Jack gave him a push and sat on him. Manny pulled the man's hands behind him and tied them while another tied his feet. They were working well as a team.

Then a shout came from the lodge, one man was getting away.

"Frank, hit the lights!" Shouted Rafe.

Jack jumped up, sprinting after the man. It was the one who had signed for the shipment and he had a gun in his hand. Jack was almost to him, when the man turned and fired! The bullet hit Jack in the arm.

"That jerk shot me!" Jack momentarily stopped, then in a burst of angered energy started after him. The older fat man was no match even for an injured Jack. Jack tackled the man around the knees and they went down with a loud "Ouf". The gun went flying. They struggled, but Jack was mad and injured arm or not, this guy wasn't getting away!

Manny, Rafe and another man came running up to assist Jack. They tied the foreman up and pushed him over to the rest of the men tied up men.

Blood had soaked Jack's shirt and was dripping down his left arm. "Hey, any of you have a scarf you can spare; I could use it for a very large Band-Aid right now."

His request was interrupted by the arrival of a white van pulling into the yard with yet another cousin at the wheel and Contessa sitting in front as a passenger.

Jack spoke out loud, "Now how on earth did she pull that one off, talking Granny into letting her come?"

They helped her out of the van and carried her to the mansion, Aunty Kate and granny got out of the back seat. Someone else got a rag from the van and they wrapped Jack's arm. He followed everyone into the mansion.

"Cray, shut off the lights." Contessa said, and quietly crooned the song.

> "Merry merry little star,
> you are so close, yet so far.
> Gone in daylight, back at night,
> basking near the fire light."

Everyone looked at the at the door, and followed the moon beam coming through the star etched window and reflected on the mirror above the fireplace then back on the star shaped brass studs above the door.

"See there, that is the answer to the song!" Contessa gleefully clapped her hands.

"Someone, turn on the lights. I think the doors are about twelve feet tall. There should be a ladder in the shed. I'll go get it, and then we can check out the frame!" Rafe spoke excitedly.

Moments later, Rafe returned with the ladder. There was a hush in the hall, suspense mounting as he placed the ladder securely against the wall, and quickly climbed up. Reaching over, he ran his hand along the top and side of the door frame. There it was a small lever the size of a ten penny nail! He turned and looked at everyone. They were all holding their breath. Slowly he pushed it to one side and heard the clicking noise as the panel next to the door frame opened a wee bit. He reached inside and pulled on the handle that was there releasing the hidden compartment door.

Six inches deep, four feet long and three feet wide, with five shelves, and on the top shelf was the leather bound pouch. There were also other papers and some small boxes.

Rafe looked down at them all and held up the leather pouch. Cheers exploded. Contessa held her clasped hands against her chest, a huge smile covering her face.

Climbing down the ladder, Rafe went to the chair Contessa was sitting in and handed her the pouch. "You open it sister, you're the one who remembered the words and figured out what the rhyme meant."

With trembling fingers, Contessa untied the strings and raised the flap of the pouch. Slowly she withdrew the old preserved paper, and handed it for Cray to read.

Cray glanced at both sides and gave them a beaming smile. "This is it! And for some strange reason our Grandpère had it signed by the judge. It is perfectly legal! We can come back home as soon as we get Auntie Kate to put a blessing on the land and buildings!"

There was excitement and joy and they were all clapping one another on their backs and giving bear hugs. It had been a long time coming, and the whole extended family was coming home!

Cray put up his hands for silence. "I know everyone is happy, but we do need to call the police and have these men questioned and at least held for trespassing until we can figure out who is the man behind everything. Rafe, climb back up there and get the rest of the items and close the compartment up. We need to get Jack's arm looked at."

All eyes turned to Jack; his left arm was covered in red blood, and a very pale face. And then for Jack…everything went black.

CHAPTER 25

Jack felt embarrassed dressed in a borrowed nightshirt with all the family around. Well, the bayou family he inherited. Auntie Kate and Granny had bathed him, cleaned his wound and wrapped it and were forcing him to take some horrible tasting stuff. Evidently the bullet went clean through his arm, missing the bone. Using their herbs, his arm had never seen so much attention. Then this bitter concoction they made him drink was suppose to build his blood back up and fight infection. Where was penicillin when you needed it? Man, was he ever glad his tetanus shot was up to date. No one thought seeing a doctor was necessary with Auntie Kate and Granny in attendance.

He could smell the incense burning, and imagined Auntie Kate had been praying and chanting for him, like she had Contessa.

"Ah, Rafe. I appreciate being taken care of and all, but do you think I could get to my truck or at least my cell phone. I need to call my company or they will have the police out looking for me and the truck. Plus, I want to call my family and I need some clothes to wear." Jack indicated the nightshirt.

"You mean this?" Rafe handed him the cell phone. "Well, my friend, your company is aware that you are here and that you've been injured. Until a town doctor gives you the okay, you can't drive. We took the liberty of bringing your phone, some clothes from your truck and the food you had there. It goes bad pretty fast in this heat." Rafe picked up the travel bag and sat it down next to Jack.

"Thank you Rafe. I really appreciate this."

Rafe nodded and handed Jack his phone. Without being told, everyone went outside to give him some privacy, such as there is on a small houseboat.

Jack called his folks first. They had just made it home. It was cold and they had been shoveling snow.

"Dad, remember how I called you and asked for a special prayer because of the load I had to deliver in New Orleans? Well, God heard them." Jack went on to relate to his Dad all that had transpired. Before Jack hung up, he said, "I love you Dad. Thanks for being you."

His next call was to Rosie. Jack never realized how much he cared about her until he got shot. She was special and he missed her.

She answered on the third ring.

"Hey Rosie, you aren't going to believe what happened to me. I got shot in the arm!"

"Jack, are you serious? Don't joke with me like that. Did you really? Are you okay? What happened? Where are you?" Rosie's voice kept going higher and louder. Her heart was pounding furiously. She couldn't bear the thought of something happening to Jack.

Jack gave her a short version of what had transpired since he left her place. "Rosie, I was wondering if you would want to fly here to New Orleans and spend some time with me for about a week. I have to stay here until the doctor gives me the okay to drive again. We could have a nice vacation and you could meet this wonderful bayou family that has been so good to me. Besides, I've missed you terribly."

Rosie couldn't believe her ears. Jack missed her and wanted her there! "Jack, be honest with me. Are you really okay? It hasn't been that long since you were in the hospital out here."

"I'm fine, Rosie. Really. I just have to let the arm heal up. Will you come? Please? I've been thinking about you a lot." Jack's voice was warm and gentle.

Rosie melted with the tone of his voice. "Yes. I'll be there as soon as I can pack and make arrangements. I'll call you with the arrival time. Where will I find you?" Rosie made up her mind quickly. Jack didn't realize how special he was to her.

"Don't worry about finding me, pretty lady. You'll recognize me; I'll be the one with the arm in the sling and a big smile on his face. And Rosie," Jack's voice husky, "This means so much to me."

Jack shut off his phone. This being alone wasn't good.

One by one, the family members came back in.

"Ho, ho. Me thinks our Jack here has a special lady. She makes you have a happy heart. You do good to keep her." Auntie Kate chuckled. "The spirits tell me."

Jack smiled at her. "You're right, Auntie Kate, she does give me a happy heart. Rafe, will you get me to town so I can line up some hotel rooms and be there when she flies in?"

"No problem my friend. We'll all go to meet this Rosie of yours and take her bags to the hotel, but then my friend, you both come back here for a special meal at the mansion. We celebrate! To the good life!"

Jack felt very blessed as he looked at his new circle of friends.

CHAPTER 26

Rosie's heart was beating furiously as she walked off the plane and scanned the sea of heads for Jack. What if she had read more into his request that she come here than he meant it to be? What if his injury was more than he told her? She twisted the shoulder strap of her purse.

Then she spotted him. Her Jack with his left arm in a sling, his right hand holding a huge bouquet of flowers, and the biggest warmest smile on his face. He was surrounded by a group of happy people holding a sign. WELCOME ROSIE.

She smiled and waved, just seeing Jack brought her racing heart almost back to normal.

Jack swiftly closed the distance between them and tried to give her a hug, but the sling got in the way.

"Let me Jack," Rosie said. Leaning against his right side, she put her arms around him and hugged him tight.

Jack leaned down and kissed her. It felt so natural.

She kissed him back with warmth. She had waited a long time for that kiss.

The clapping of hands and whistles got the young couple's attention.

Rosie's face turned as pink as the roses in the bouquet.

Leaving his good arm around her waist, Jack cleared his throat, "Rosie, come meet my new friends." He then proceeded to introduce them starting with Granny, the eldest.

She touched Rosie's cheek. "Any friend or kin of Jack's is our friend and welcomed here." Granny gave her instant approval of Rosie.

Next was Auntie Kate. Taking both of Rosie's hands in hers, she gazed into the young woman's happy blue eyes. She smiled then, her white teeth sparkling against her ebony skin. She embraced Rosie warmly then stepped back, still holding her hands said, "You be good for young Jack. The spirits tell me."

Rosie threw Jack a bewildered look, not knowing how to take this bit of fortune telling.

Jack gave Rosie a warm squeeze to reassure her. "Auntie Kate is a good judge of character. I think you're good for me too."

Contessa, Manny, Rafe, and Clay were introduced to Rosie. They swiftly accepted each other, and new friendships were started.

Manny and Rafe each picked up a suitcase and Clay led the way to the white van. After everyone was settled in the vehicle, Clay drove to the quaint old hotel Jack had booked rooms in. They all trooped in to inspect first Rosie's room and then Jack's. The men stood back and let the four women comment on the charming furnishings and beautiful view from the windows. Satisfied with the rooms, the women joined the men.

Contessa spoke, "You both know you're more than welcome to stay with us on the houseboats. The mansion will be ready in two more days. The furniture is in place and we are ordering the food. You will come out then for the day and stay the night. We are having a huge party to celebrate the blessing on the mansion and land. All the family will be there and many friends. Music, dancing and plenty of food, there is nothing like a Cajun party!"

"That sounds like fun! I can't wait. Everything is different here; there is so much to see. Why don't you join us in some sightseeing?" Rosie replied.

Rafe laughed, "We have much to get done and you two need some time together. Jack, you take it easy and don't over-due it. Be careful where you go at night. Not every area of the town is safe. We'll come and get you in two days. Here is the number for the phone at the mansion if you need anything. Don't worry about your truck. It will be watched." Rafe stretched out his hand to shake Jack's.

They all said their good-byes and started for the door when Auntie Kate turned her large body around very slowly and pointed her finger at the young couple, "No hankie pankie stuff, bring bad luck. The spirits will tell me." Then she left.

Jack walked over and closed the door.

"Whew, what do you think about that?" Rosie asked with a nervous laugh.

Jack pulled her down next to him on the loveseat. "Rosie, let me tell you about the bayou people. They are a mixture of French, Indian, African, and who knows what else. They have a belief in God, but also a mixture of many other beliefs. You'd be amazed at the ESP they used and the knowledge in herbs, the land, and animals. They have very generous hearts. But don't cross them." Then Jack told her all that had transpired from Reno to being shot.

"Unbelievable. It sounds like a story someone made up! But what about your arm, have you seen a doctor Jack? I'm not totally sold on all that medicine from the bayou." Rosie gently touched his left arm.

"Yes I have company policy you know. The funny thing about that visit, the doctor said he couldn't have done any better, and if Auntie Kate would get a patent on half of her concoctions, she could be a rich woman. Evidently, I'm not the first person to see the doctor after she has done her magic with healing herbs first."

"How long will you have to wear the sling? What about your work?"

"The doc recommended using the sling in public mainly to keep people from bumping into me. I can take it off otherwise and move it around. He doesn't want it to get stiff on me. As for work, I'm taking this week off as vacation. Legally, I can't say it was Workman's Comp. I didn't have to get involved with the takeover at the mansion. But personally, I did have to help

Contessa, work or no work. As for the truck being idle this week, the dispatcher knew I didn't want to take this load, I had an eerie feeling about it. No one is making any waves." Jack smiled at her. "So, what say we go find a nice restaurant within walking distance and enjoy our time together?" Jack leaned over and ever so gently kissed her.

Wrapping her arms around his neck, Rosie returned his kiss. It felt so good and right. Then she pulled back, smiled and stood up. Reaching out for his hand she said, "Come on, I'm famished. If we stay here hugging and kissing, Auntie Kate might just appear. Remember the warning, 'no hanky-panky'."

Laughing, they locked the door and headed for the stairs. During their meal, they would plan their week, well at least two days worth. Then they had the mansion party, and that could change their plans for the rest of the week.

* * *

The two days passed swiftly as the young couple in their newly found love visited museums, graveyards, and went on horse drawn carriage rides. Everything seemed magical, the colors brighter, the street vendor's wares tempting them to try something new. They went shopping and bought gifts for Jack's family, and friends. Jack made sure he picked out a real nice rust colored shirt for Rafe. They found the perfect lavender silk scarf for Auntie Kate. New soft cushions of varying shades of blue for Granny's rocking chair that matched the new slippers they bought her. Rosie found a small crystal figurine of an angel and Jack agreed that was perfect gift for Contessa. She must have angels working overtime protecting her. For Manny and Cray, they purchased colorful neck scarves that the men wore.

They had time to sit and visit. They discovered their friendship was more serious than they thought.

"Rosie, with all that has transpired since I left after Christmas, it made me realize how special you are to me. You're strong, yet all woman."

"Jack, the first time you walked into the truck stop, something happened to me. At first I thought it was your handsome looks, but it was more. I didn't know if you felt anything or not. When you came to my rescue during the attempted robbery, I felt you were more concerned about me than just helping a damsel in distress. I won't ever forget your bout with pneumonia and we had all that recovery time together, I...I didn't want you to leave. When you kissed me at your truck, I knew I wanted more than friendship."

Jack held her tightly and murmured into her hair, "I wasn't sure of how much was the magic of the season. I must be the biggest lunk head around."

She laughed and relaxed in his embrace. Then she pulled back, linking arms with him said, "I think we have some more shopping to do." She needed to walk and she was too full of emotions to sit still.

As they strolled through the many shops, Rosie was intrigued by a simple very old light blue opal ring entwined in a delicately twisted gold band.

Jack never said a thing, but he had observed her interest in the ring. Then she moved along to other displays.

"Rosie, excuse me for a minute while I find the gentleman's room." Jack started walking to the back of the shop.

He caught the attention of the shopkeeper. "My friend is looking at the opal in a gold setting. How much is it?"

The owner gave Jack an affordable price.

Jack nodded to him. "I'll take it. Deliver it to my hotel this evening about five, and I'll pay for it then. This is a surprise for the lady, so please don't say anything." Jack wrote down the name and room number of the hotel he was staying at.

Joining Rosie once more, Jack took her hand and they strolled out of the shop. Jack felt like jumping in the air and clicking his heels. He smiled. Little did Rosie know that tonight would be special. Very special.

CHAPTER 27

Jack and Rosie had dinner on the veranda of the quaint old hotel. In the gentle breeze, the colorful flowers scented the area with light fragrances. It was a perfect night with stars twinkling in the blue velvet sky. In the main dining room the sounds of the trio playing romantic songs floated softly out to them.

The meal was a culinary delight, but tonight it was wasted on Jack. He ate without appreciating the fine food. He had other things on his mind; like a blue eyed, red headed beauty sitting across from him.

"Rosie. I, ah, how important is your truckers business with Carl?" Jack was nervous, his heart was beating overtime.

"Jack honey, you know I've worked very hard to make the Trucker's Stop a growing business, patronized by truckers and travelers alike. I guess it has taken up my time that normally people devote to family. When Sara and Brian leave for Wisconsin, I'll really feel lonely."

He reached out and took her hands, "Would you feel lonely if you sold out to Carl and became my wife?"

"Your wife?" Rosie whispered, her blue eyes wide with surprise. *Did she really hear Jack say 'wife'?*

As if Jack had heard her question, he reached in his pocket taking out the box with the opal ring and knelt down in front of her. "I never realized how much I loved you until the night I was shot. You were the first person I thought of. I want to be with you Rosie, take care of you. I'm lonely without you. Will you marry me?"

Tears were wetting her cheeks as she answered. "Jack, the first time I ever laid eyes on you, I felt something. Maybe it was that chemistry everyone talks about. I have loved you for so long but didn't think you knew it." She wiped the tears from her face and smiled at him. "When you were sick in the hospital, I never felt so afraid in all my life. Then, I didn't how Sara fit in your life, so I tried to stay in the background. And now to know that you love me too...Yes, my darling! I would be proud to be your wife!"

Jack slipped the delicate blue opal on her finger and they sealed the answer with a kiss.

Through her misty eyes, she gazed lovingly at the special ring on her finger. The very same ring she thought was so beautiful at the little shop they had visited earlier. Never in a hundred years would she have entertained the thought that it would become her engagement ring.

She put her arms around Jack's neck and hugged him close. "You've made me so happy and honored, Jack." Rosie kissed him as only a young woman in love can, passionately.

The waiter observing this marriage proposal went to the trio and requested a special love song.

Jack and Rosie, happy in love, danced and smiled as only a couple experiencing that wondrous moment of declared love can. It was a magical night they would remember for the rest of their lives.

* * *

Arms entwined, moving as one, Jack and Rosie climbed the stairs to their rooms.

"Rosie, I would like to call and tell my folks that you accepted to be my bride and I'm the happiest man in the world!" Jack picked her up and twirled her around, before slowly letting her down. Not releasing her, Jack held her close and kissed her tenderly on the lips.

"Um, it's pretty late Jack." She trailed some kisses across his cheek, ending on his lips. "We might wake them."

He kissed her back. "I don't think they will mind. It's not every day they learn they're to be in-laws again."

They went to the phone and Jack placed the call.

His mom answered. "Hello."

"Hi Mom, it's me Jack."

"Oh Jack!" She called out, "Bob, it's Jack." Speaking back into the phone, "Are you okay dear? Is your arm bothering you?" Concern filled her voice.

"Everything's fine Mom. I'm glad you're both still up. I have some wonderful news to share."

Jack could hear his mother calling his Dad to pick up the other phone.

"What's up Jack, you never call this late." Bob's low voice came on the line.

"I never had such happy news before!" Excitement filled his voice. "Mom, Dad, Rosie just agreed to be my wife and we wanted you both to be the first to know!"

"What? Rosie is there with you? What a surprise! Congratulations son! We couldn't be happier for you both. Let me talk with Rosie."

Jack handed the phone to Rosie.

"Hello, I'm thrilled that Jack asked me to be his wife!" Rosie spoke happily into the phone, laughing and crying at the same time.

Alice and Bob both started to speak at the same time and they all laughed.

"Mother and I couldn't have picked out a better lady for our son. We welcome you into our family!" Bob's voice was sincere.

Alice's voice was choked up and they could hear the tears as she spoke. "I'm finally getting you for my daughter. I grew to love you when we got acquainted at Christmas. It seems natural for you to be Jack's wife. When did this all transpire? Where are you? Have you set a date?" The questions came in rapid succession.

Rosie and Jack had the phone between them and heard his mother's question. "Well Mom, we haven't got that far. It hasn't been that long since I dusted off my knee from proposing to Rosie." He leaned over and gave Rosie a kiss on her perky nose.

Bob came back on the line. "I'll let Daniel and Sara, and your sister know, unless you want to call them."

"No, that's fine dad. You tell them. We will call you back tomorrow when we've had time to plan and sort out details. Night folks."

"Good night you two. You have made Dad and me very happy with the news." Alice said.

Both couples hung up.

Rosie and Jack stood there, gazing at one another, lost in the magical moment. The music from downstairs drifted up through their open balcony.

Taking her into his arms, the two slowly danced. Jack didn't want to let her go, she felt so warm in his arms. His heart was pounding with all the love he felt for her.

Finally, Rosie stopped and looking up at Jack with loved filled eyes said, "I think my darling that we had better come off cloud nine. If I remember right, Manny or Rafe is going to pick us up tomorrow about noon to help out at the mansion for the festivities. As much as I love being in your arms, I need some beauty sleep. We need to pack for the dinner and dance. I can't wait until we are married, but for now, good-night my love." Rosie kissed him gently on the lips, but didn't move a muscle.

"You're right Rosie. I hate to see the night end; you fit in my arms like they were made for you. And my dear, for the record, you don't need any beauty sleep. You're the most beautiful woman in the world." Jack held her tightly, his face resting against her soft auburn hair.

Rosie started to chuckle, "Jack, with all of Auntie Kate's spirits, I wonder if she will know we are going to be married before we tell her!"

Jack laughed with her, then he sobered up. "That really isn't so funny, Rosie. The people who live back in the bayou are different. Let's not say anything tomorrow until we are all dressed and ready for the party. If no one says anything until we announce it, then we know that Auntie Kate's spirits were sleeping tonight."

Rosie nodded her head in agreement.

Jack opened the door to his room, blew her a kiss and closed the door.

Rosie put out her arms and spun around, then fell backwards on the bed. She was going to be Mrs. Jack O'Ryan! There was so much to plan, but for tonight, she was going to replay every special moment of the last wonderful two days. She wished her folks were alive so she could tell them how happy she was.

Slowly she got off the bed and walked out to the balcony. Looking up at the stars said out loud, "Mom, Dad, did you hear the news? Your Rosie is going to marry the most handsome, wonderful man in the world."

Peacefulness settled over her. She was sure that was her parents blessing. Now she could go to bed and sleep. Her dreams filled with bridal gowns, flowers, and Jack.

CHAPTER 28

Ironically, it was the same time of the day when they entered the small road that lead to the mansion as it was a week ago when Jack arrived with the semi full of furniture. For some reason the silver moss laden branches overhead didn't produce the apprehension and coils of unrest in Jack as they did that late afternoon. Today they seemed to welcome him and it seemed cozy. Or maybe, it seemed that way because he had his arm around the woman he loved.

Manny glanced into the rearview mirror at the young couple and chuckled silently to himself. If he could read signs at all, he would predict wedding bells in the future, the *very* near future.

Pulling in to the mansion grounds, Jack stared with utter disbelief! Gone were the overgrowth of trees and weeds. The buildings had undergone a transformation with painting and fixing. The parking area was full of vehicles from chauffeur driven limousines to horses munching hay in the corral.

Manny stopped the van, turned around in his seat and looked back at the bewildered Jack. "We have been busy for the last week, oui, my friend?"

"I guess you have. Are you sure we're in the right place?" Jack smiled back at him. Visions of the gunfight not that long ago, came to his mind.

Manny flashed his smile, "I am sure my friend. Come, Auntie Kate will bless the land and remove the curse. It is time to celebrate with our many family and friends, from the town and the inner parts of the bayou!"

Manny opened the sliding door of the van and reached for Rosie's hand and helped her down. Jack followed close behind.

As they entered the mansion hall, Rosie felt like she had stepped into another era. All the women were dressed in stunning gowns, the men in tuxedos. She was glad she had worn the beautiful sea foam green filmy dress.

Granny wore a silk blue dress with a matching jacket and Contessa in a simple but elegant white gown with a lacy shawl were greeting the guests. Auntie Kate stood behind them, part family, part protector, splendid in a golden turban and bronze colored outfit. She reminded Rosie of ancient royalty.

The rosy hue of the sun was ebbing into sunset.

"The time is now." Auntie Kate said to Granny.

Manny stepped up to the microphone and motioned to the local band dressed in black pants, red cummerbunds, and white peasants shirts, to stop playing.

"Ladies and Gentlemen. The family welcomes each and every one of you to this celebration of healing. Auntie Kate will now ask the spirits and God to remove the curse and bless this land, so once more our families will prosper and be happy. Auntie Kate." Manny gestured with his arm to her.

She bowed slightly towards him in acknowledgement. Then taking Granny by the arm, Auntie Kate regally led the procession through the huge wooden double doors to the courtyard. Contessa, Manny, Cray, and all the rest of the guests silently followed her. Auntie Kate stopped in the middle of the clearing where a huge pile of wood was laid ready to burn. The sun had disappeared and they were now in the twilight. It was time. She motioned for Cray to start the fire.

Quietly, reverently, everyone gathered in a circle around the crackling fire. The atmosphere could be described as being in an outdoor cathedral. Blessings and healings were holy to them.

Auntie Kate bowed her head and hands clasped against her ample bosom was silently praying. Suddenly she threw her arms up in the air, saying in a clear voice that all could hear, "Almighty Father, Spirits of the day, Spirits of the night, we come together to remove the evil from this place." Then she slowly walked to her left around the fire.

Each time she completed the circle, she withdrew from the small bag attached by a satin cord around her expanded waist, a small piece of material or another object associated with the people, land and house. Raising her arm high, she would say, "Be gone evil. Father God, bless this land," and throw the article in the fire with exuberance, making sparks fly. When the bag was empty, she threw that in also, producing an unexpected loud bang.

Everyone watched as the flames licked around the objects, destroying them.

The huge fire cast eerie shadows over the faces of the people on the other side of the circle. Rosie shuddered and tightened her grip on Jack's hand. She watched this strange ritual with curiosity and fear. *Was this Cajun voodoo or some type of Christianity that she wasn't aware of?*

Rosie glanced over at Jack, receiving reassurance that he would never put her in harm's way. Not her 'Warrior of the Road' Jack.

Jack feeling her eyes on him smiled down at her and gently squeezed her hand. He thought Rosie was so very, very, beautiful with the dancing firelight highlighting her features and giving her hair a rich, shimmering copper glow.

Then Auntie Kate took Granny's hand and motioned for everyone to join hands. As one the circle of people approached the fire with raised hands as Auntie Kate called out with emotion, "Father God, bless the people, bless the land."

Everyone said, "Amen" as they bowed and backed up.

Seven times the group circled the fire, surged forward and then fell back as Auntie Kate prayed, "Father God, bless the people, bless the land," and they all responded as one, "Amen".

At the last 'Amen', a flash of lightning appeared out of nowhere filling the night with light. Then the sky became a velvet black ceiling dotted with an endless showering of stars.

In reverence, Auntie Kate called out, "Thank you Father God, thank you Spirits of the land, for healing this place. May we be good stewards of it and live in harmony." Silently she stood there, in private communication with God, her face turned to the heavens, the firelight bringing out the gold in her turban she wore, giving her an angelic appearance. Slowly, she turned around, "The land is now free and blessed."

Once more taking Granny's arm, she with dignity lead the quiet group of people to the mansion with the lights ablaze, welcoming them back.

Jack and Rosie stayed behind, watching the fire.

Rosie clung to Jack's hand, not quite sure what to make of the whole thing. She had been raised as a conservative Christian. All this good spirits, evil spirits she had just witnessed didn't fit in with her belief. God was the Almighty. Yet, she had felt a spiritual power with positive energies here.

Jack didn't know what to make of it either. Was God okay with this? He wished his dad was here, he had a stronger relationship with God than Jack did. He recalled a scripture about calling on Him with faith believing... and Jack remembered in St. Luke, chapter eight, Jesus commanded the unclean spirits out of the wild man and they entered the swine and the swine ran violently into the lake and were drowned. In this case, it seemed the evil perished in the fire.

He looked back at the dying embers of the fire. "Rosie, this extended family plans on using this land for the good of them all. I think God will bless them. A prayer is a prayer, inside a church, in the great outdoors or in the stillness of our silent meditation."

He took her in his arms and held her close. "Come on beautiful, let's go join the party and see if Auntie Kate has guessed we are going to get married."

***

Jack and Rosie stood at the entrance of the hall, not quite sure where to go. People mingling through the rooms on both sides of the huge vestibule full of beautiful flower arrangements and the sound of lively music floating through the air setting a festive atmosphere.

Manny motioned for them to enter the room where a huge buffet was set up. Granny presided at the head table; seated with her were Contessa, Auntie Kate, Cray, Manny and their families. There were also seats for Rosie and Jack.

"Fill your plates then join us on the rostrum." Manny told them gesturing at the vast amount of food.

Rosie and Jack were over whelmed with the selection of mouthwatering dishes displayed. Jack wondered if all the food was prepared by relatives or if they were brought in by special caterers. His stomach growled and he wasted no time filling his plate.

Auntie Kate sat next to Rosie and poured tea into Rosie's cup. "When you are finished drinking your tea, I shall read your future."

Rosie looked over at Jack. *Whatever happened to tea bags?*

He smiled back at her and squeezed her hand reassuring her everything was alright.

They were finishing their meal when waiters brought glasses of champagne and placed them in front of everyone.

Manny motioned to the band and they gave a drum roll. There was total silence in the huge ballroom.

"Family, friends, and honored guests. Once more the mansion welcomes you one and all with open arms. This has been possible with the blessings of God and the help of our family and friends. If it had not been for our dear friend, Jack O'Ryan, our special Contessa would not be here to celebrate with us and the curse of evil would still be on this land." Turning to face Jack, "You saved my dear sister's life, for this we are deeply grateful." Manny bowed to Jack, then he raising his glass of champagne in a salute, "To Jack O'Ryan!"

"To Jack O'Ryan!" The rousing cheer and thunderous applause from the assembled guests left no doubt of their feelings for the young man and his actions.

Jack's face got red. He didn't expect this. He looked around for an escape route, and in doing so, saw the genuine look of respect, honor, and thankfulness on each and every face. His urge to leave was over. That is how he would have felt had it been his sister, Deb. He glanced down at Rosie who reached up her hand and squeezed his conveying how proud she was of this brave man she loved.

Manny continued, "This evening, we make him an honorary member of the bayou family, and we also have a check for fifty thousand dollars to compensate for his lost wages as he recovers from his injury received for helping save our Contessa and the inheritance of our mansion and land."

Manny paused momentarily overcome with emotion. Taking a breath with a huge smile on his face spoke with a clear voice, "To my dear friend, Jack and his intended, Rosie, our token of appreciation." Manny bowed and handed the envelope to Jack. Giving Jack a manly hug, he kissed both sides of Jack's face as the other guests stood and cheered. The Contessa was well loved by them all. Now, Jack was their hero.

Jack stood quietly unable to speak as he tried to absorb this tribute given to him by these gracious people. Tears wet his face. Wiping his hand across his eyes, he gestured for everyone to sit down. Then he bowed to everyone at the table, "I am very humbled by this show of affection." He raised the envelope in the air. "I can't take the money. I never helped Contessa for any money. She was in need. That is how I was raised, to assist others. I thank you from the bottom of my heart for this tribute, to be part of your family, but I can't take the money."

Auntie Kate stood up and with her usual take charge attitude walked over to Jack and placed her hand on his shoulder. They stood eye to eye, "Honey chile, you shorenuf can. You and your sweet lady can use it for a wedding trip."

Rosie and Jack's mouths fell open with surprise. She did know!

"The spirits tell me, no hankie pinkie going on here, but true love." She turned toward Rosie. "I read your tea leaves and I see three babies for you." Auntie Kate smiled at the two.

Jack sat down with a thud. Mercifully, the band began to play and the dance floor filled up with happy couples.

So, when you two jump the broom?" Auntie Kate asked. At their puzzled looks, she added, "Get married?"

Smiling at Rosie, Jack replied, "Soon. Very soon.

CHAPTER 29

Rosie tapped her pen against the notebook, "These last ten months have been a whirl wind. Are we really going to be ready for the wedding in two days?" She looked around the wooden table at Jack, Daniel and Sara who also had their note pads in front of them.

Taking a drink of his coffee, Jack smiled at her, "We could just jump the broom like Auntie Kate said. Relax honey, the tux are here, your dresses made it, and," he touched the ivory colored envelope, "Our marriage license is here. I got my part of this taken care of."

Rosie gently threw a wadded napkin at him. "What about the mansion and the bayou family? You didn't forget about that part I hope?" She laughed at him. There was no way *he would forget those arrangements.*

"You can cross that off your list too. Travel arrangements done thanks to Dad's friend."

"I forgot to tell you that I had a strange conversation with Manny last night. I should say, Auntie Kate. She had him place the call. She told me 'the spirits tell her we need to double check everything', and that she would have special prayers for us. Then she hung up."

"Wow that sounds spooky. Are you sure we should go there? Yah know, big brother, I've never met these bayou people. Let's cancel going there. All in favor raise your right hand." Daniel had a look of concern on his face.

Rosie laughed, "Now you know how I felt when I first met them. But they are good people and have a mixture of Christianity and who knows what will transpire. We will be safe there. Don't be a worry wart."

With a doubtful look, Sara looked around the table at everyone, "You said she reads tea leaves, maybe she misinterpreted some of them."

"Come one, relax everyone; I guess I shouldn't have said anything." Jack laughed, "But...for the next two days, no one walks under a ladder okay. For now back to everyone's list."

"I guess we had the easy part," Sara added taking a hold of Daniel's hand. The invitations were all sent out, and the RSVP list is here." She touched a folder that held the names and addresses.

"Man, I'm really glad we decided to have a double wedding! I never knew how much work there was to all of this. It's a good thing the family has helped us with the planning. I'm getting nervous. I think your Auntie Kate might be on to something with that jumping the broom bit."

Daniel stood up and walked around the table and poured himself another cup of coffee. "At least I have my college degree in business management," stopping next to Rosie, he put his hand on her shoulder, "And thanks to you, Sara and I will be part owners of a thriving business."

Continuing around the table to sit next to Sara, "I'm really looking forward to us getting married, it just seems like it turned into more than I imagined. Maybe we should elope."

"I don't think so, brother of mine." Deb stood with her arms crossed leaning against the dining room archway. "I didn't buy myself and the girls some fancy duds and not be able to wear them."

Pushing herself away from the wall, she joined them by the dining room table. She started to count on her fingers, "The church is reserved, the organist music picked, the soloist, the florist, the pastor, the caterer, and our plane and reservations for the hotel in New Orleans are all taken care. Did I forget anything?" She reached for a cookie and joined them at the table.

"It's going to be a long day for the kids though, but they can sleep on the plane. It would be nice if the bayou family could have come here for the ceremony, but I realize that is a lot for Granny and Auntie Kate." Rosie continued, "I bet we are the first ones to have a wedding at 11:00 AM, lunch immediately after the ceremony for the guests, change into something comfy, pack our wedding clothes, and be on the plane and at the bayou by six. It sure was nice of your dad's friend to fly us all down with his company plane or we would have had to make it much later."

"For some reason it was important to them we have that celebration at the mansion the same day as the wedding. I suppose it is a Cajun superstition or something like that." Jack added shrugging his shoulders.

"I'm glad we are going to be witnesses for each other. It's not every day that brothers get married at the same time." Sara said quietly. She had grown to love this family so much and little Brian was crazy about Daniel and had started calling him daddy.

"The biggest surprise to me was when Rosie went to the truck driving school and got her CDL. Are you two really sure you want to team drive?" Deb asked them her eyes full of curiosity, "That is a lot of togetherness; sure you won't get on each other's nerves?"

"Since I sold my half of the business to Daniel and Sara, and they will be living in my house, I don't want to wait at Jack's apartment hoping he will make it home every weekend. And I'm use to being busy. Besides, look at all the people he meets and places I've never been, and now we can do it together. I can't wait." Rosie's eyes were sparkling with excitement.

They were interrupted by the phone ringing. Deb answered it. "Yes, Jack is here, one moment please." She curled her finger at Jack.

"Hello. Jack, here."

"Hey, Jack my boy. I should be pulling into your town tomorrow afternoon. Where do I park my rig?" Lou's voice wasn't so low and husky since she quit smoking.

"I'm so glad you can make it, I was afraid you wouldn't be able to as busy as you are."

Laughing Lou commented, "You didn't think for a moment I'd miss the wedding of my tea drinking friend and Rosie."

"For the record, Lou, I do drink more coffee now. Ah Lou, did you cut back on all that potatoes and gravy, and the gallon of cream to your rot gut coffee?" Jack liked teasing her.

"Don't smart off to me, boy, or I'll take my present back."

"I'll be good. Call me when you are coming off the interstate, I'll meet you at the mall and you can follow me to the company parking lot where I leave mine. I'll get you a temporary pass since it is a secured lot. I've okayed it with the boss. Gosh I'm sure glad you made it in time. If it is okay with you, I planned on you staying at my apartment with Sara and her little boy. Since Rosie and I have been engaged, I've stayed at my sister's place when I'm in town. I hope you brought some pictures of the baby." Jack never doubted for a minute that Lou wouldn't make it for the wedding.

"I sure do. Matter of fact I've got quite a few. Grandma's do that you know, carry a small photo book around." Lou's voice was happy. "See you tomorrow, Jack." And with that, she hung up.

Replacing the phone, Jack looked over at Sara, "Your roomy for the next two days will be in town tomorrow. That was Lou."

"Do you realize that tomorrow evening is the dress rehearsal? Do we really need to do that? I might faint." Daniel was laughing as he feigned passing out. "Besides we have relatives that will be at the hotel that we should visit with, it's gonna be a lot of excitement for the girls and Brian."

"Oh you," Rosie said, "We won't be long at the church for the rehearsal, since we just have ourselves and Katie and Mira our flower girls, and little Brian will carry the rings. We can leave the marriage license with the pastor. That's a nice thing about having a small wedding party. We will just walk through it and then meet the relatives at the hotel and have the pizza party. Then home early for beddy-bye."

The phone rang again and Deb answered. "We are on our way."

She turned to the group, "That was mom; supper is ready so we better hurry up since the kids are hungry."

They didn't have to be told a second time and they all hurried to their vehicles. Mom was such a great cook.

* * *

The soloist had sung their chosen song, and now the organist was softly playing when the pastor smiled at Jack and Daniel. "Ready?"

Both of the men nodded, even though the butterflies in their stomach were doing summersaults.

The two grooms nervously waited until the pastor reached his place and indicated with his head for them to follow. They slowly walked out and turned to face the congregation, family and friends. They watched as the usher walked their mom down the aisle and seated her with Joe, Deb, Lou and Carl in the front pew.

Jack rubbed his finger inside his collar. It sure was getting warm in here.

Daniel was wishing he had a drink of water, his mouth felt full of cotton.

The two brothers smiled as they watched Mira and Katie in their petty new frilly dresses scatter flower petals from their baskets as they walked toward them. Little Brian followed close behind clutching onto the white pillow that held the rings with a tight grip. They could tell the way he marched wearing his big boy white suit he was feeling oh so important. And then, the music changed and the double doors opened wide.

Daniel and Jack both took a sharp breath at how beautiful their soon to be wives were.

Rosie was dressed in a white long gown, unpretentious, but elegant. On her head was a round small hat with seedless pearls sewn around the edges. She wore a pair of pearl earrings that had been her mothers.

Sara was wearing a strapless white gown with a full skirt. Her hair was swept up with a single flower in it. She wore no jewelry.

Bob, with Sara on one arm and Rosie on the other walking slowly in time to the music made their way to the front of the church, stopping in front of the pastor.

"Who gives these women to marry?" The pastor asked.

At that moment, Deb, Joe, Alice, and Carl stood up and Bob looked over at them and together they said, "We do."

There was smiles and soft laughter from the guests.

Bob gave Rosie a kiss on the cheek as Jack stepped forward and took Rosie's hand. Then Bob gave Sara a kiss on her cheek as Daniel came to offer his arm for Sara. Both he and Alice loved the young women. Bob sat down with his family.

Little Brian stood in the middle between the two couples, looking up at his mom, "I walked real good, Mommy like you told me too."

"Yes you did, honey." Sara whispered to her young son giving him a gentle pat on his shoulder.

Pastor Williams smiled and began, "We have come together today to share this special wedding day of Jack and Rosie, Daniel and Sara. It isn't very often I get to marry two brothers on the same day." He raised his hand up, "Please stand for the prayer" When he finished the welcoming prayer, he told the congregation, "You may be seated."

"I have known these two boys since they were the age of Brian. Let me assure you that they always made their presence known, like ringing the church bell at the wrong time, as Christmas angels managing to knock one of their wings off during the play, and one time collapsing the tent on a camping trip. As they matured they have provided us with music and helpful hands wherever needed. And now, these two young men have matured and together with their lovely brides enter the special bond of matrimony. They have had an excellent example of a good Christian family from their parents, Bob and Alice. I want to share from the fifth chapter of Ephesians verses 20 through 31." He then expounded on the principals of family living.

At his point in the service, he had each couple repeat after him, their vows.

"Brian, may I have the rings now?" the pastor asked the little boy who had remain very still all this time still holding tightly to the white satin pillow.

"Is is okay to let go of the pillow now, mommy, Grandpa Bob said I had to keep them safe."

There was a twittering and smiles from the congregation at the young boy's question.

Leaning down she put her arm around her young son, "Yes Brian, now is the time for us to have the rings." Sara assured him.

Jack slipped the plain gold band next to the blue opal on Rosie's finger.

Sara was wearing the diamond engagement ring that Daniel had given her and he placed a wedding band that held three diamonds on her finger: one for Sara, one for Brian, and one for him, his new family.

After the couple exchanged rings, the pastor gave a prayer of blessing and pronounced them husband and wife. "You may each kiss your bride.

And the two men did with much enthusiasm.

CHAPTER 30

The little plane as Bob's friend had called it could have easily carried thirty people, but gave the extended family lots of room. There was a toilet and a small area for snacks and drinks. He had even provided an attendant for serving them.

Once they got the word they could unhook their seatbelts everyone began moving around and talking.

"Dad, did you know Mr. Swanson's plane was this big? I thought we would be sandwiched in like sardines." Jack questioned his dad.

"Not really, I know he has a small two seater that he can fly himself and he said two others. He flies all over in the businesses that he and his son own. This is nice wedding gift for you. I'd hate to pay just for the fuel on this thing. Oh, and I think I forgot to tell you, the three suites at the hotel we are staying at…those are his. Again NO CHARGE." Bob smiled. "You would never know he is rich. When we go fishing, my old stuff is newer than his. He is just a good person."

Deb spoke up, "But I made all the reservations for the hotel and they weren't suites I can tell you, not on our budgets."

"He told me not to tell all of you until we checked in, but he had your rooms changed and Deb, your credit card is no longer charged for anything." Bob's eyes were full of laughter as he saw her mouth shape into an O.

Leaning over to kiss Sara, Daniel whispered, "Honey, I didn't think Mr. Swanson had that much money! He has always just been a friend of Dad's. He was never treated like royalty or anything. Wow. Um, nice kiss."

Over the speaker the pilot spoke, "Would you sit down and put on your belts, it looks like a bit of turbulence ahead. Thank you."

There was a flurry of movement as everyone got in their seats. The stewardess walked up and down the small isle making sure they were all safely buckled in and collected any bottles of water or soda. That's when the wedding party noticed how dark the sky had become and the rain began was falling.

Ever so often they could feel the plane buck. The lightning flashed brightly at times leaving the sky like a giant ink well.

"Jack, this reminds me of the first time we met. Rain, wind, lightning and your wonderful warm truck, I think I called it the steel oasis." Sara spoke up.

"I think I like storms better when I have all eighteen wheels on the ground." Jack responded.

Rosie chimed in, "Do you think Auntie Kate meant the weather forecast when she told us to 'check' everything?"

One could feel the nervousness of everyone. Conversation ceased.

Once again, the pilot spoke on the speaker, "For some reason it shows we are losing some fuel. It could be the buffeting of the wind has cause the gauge to malfunction. There should be enough left to reach our destination, I will land in a smaller field if I deem it necessary."

Bob spoke up, "I think we need to have a little talk with the Lord. We all are apprehensive now." With that said, Bob began to pray. He prayed for the pilot, the plane, their peace of mind and a safe arrival to New Orleans.

When the last amen was heard, Bob spoke, "Brian did grandma and I tell you what a wonderful way you held on to the satin pillow with the rings in it today. You walked so nice and didn't drop it. You are really getting to be a big boy."

"It was my job, cause when Daniel put the ring on Momma's finger he told me we are all married and I was really his boy." Brian smiled at his mom and Daniel, "So, now I have a momma and a daddy. We are a family, and you are real grandpa and grandma too."

The jerking of the plane caused all conversation to stop and the lights flickered.

The speaker clicked again, "We are approaching the airport, I've radioed the tower and told them we need to land out of order, I'm losing power. Be prepared we may have a rough landing."

Everything went quiet in the plane. Those on the window seats looked out and could see the runway lights. They experienced a couple of bumps as they landed and slowly came to a stop.

Everything was still, and then the sound of breathe being exhaled. They looked at each other. They had landed safety.

Out of the stillness came Brian's voice, "That was fun, can we do it again."

Everyone began to laugh, a laugh about Brian's comment and a laugh of relief for a safe landing.

Jack unbuckled his seat belt and assisted Rosie from her seat, "I sure hope Manny and the family don't have anything exciting and unusual planned. I think I've had enough stimulation for one day."

Rosie hugged her new husband, "Oh it will be tame for them, probably something like alligator wrestling." They all smiled. The day wasn't over yet.

***

The two vans came to a stop outside the mansion and there was a flurry of excitement as Granny, Auntie Kate and Contessa were hugging and welcoming everyone. Introductions were made and Auntie Kate ordered Manny, Clay and whoever had a free hand to take the luggage upstairs and to the rooms so the families could change back into their wedding finery.

The guests were waiting, this was party time, as was popular among the Cajun people, 'laissez le bon temp rouler', or, let the good times roll.

"Jack, I can't find my wedding dress."

"Are you sure? Maybe it was taken to one of the other rooms. Let's go check." He took her hand and they knocked on the others doors but her dress was nowhere to be found.

"Let's go down stairs and see if it got left in one of the vans." They both quickly went down the winding stairway.

"Why aren't you dressed yet? Everyone waiting for your two couples to come down all dressed up." Auntie Kate had a frown on her face.

"Auntie Kate, we can't find Rosie's' wedding dress. We think perhaps it got left in one of the vans."

"No, I double checked both of them before we moved them away from the entrance. Nothing was left in them." Manny had suddenly appeared at Jack's shoulder.

Jack jumped in surprise, "Manny, you scared me half to death, I didn't hear you come up next to us."

"Jack, what should I do, I can't show up in my jeans and sweater? Do you think it might be at the hotel with the other luggage?" Rosie was ready to cry. She was tired; it had been an exhausting day and now this. Enough already.

Auntie Kate put her arms around the Rosie and hugged her tightly nearly smothering the young woman in her amble bosom, "Not to fret honey chile, now you just go back up stairs and wash your face, Auntie Kate take care of everything. Shoo now." She turned Rosie toward the stairs. Nodding at Jack, "You go to, get ready now."

With that Auntie Kate disappeared.

About five minutes later, there was a knock on Jack's door. Opening it he was surprised to see Contessa standing there holding the white dress she had worn when the blessing of the mansion was done.

"May I come in? I have a dress for Rosie."

"By all means. Rosie, come here." Jack was closing the door when…

"Wait for me", Auntie Kate came bustling into the room carrying an ornate bag. "What? Jack you ain't dressed yet?" She shook her head. "Take your clothes next door to your folk's room, we women got things to do here."

Jack didn't question her, just picked up his suit carrier and left the room. One didn't question Auntie Kate.

With Jack gone, the women went to work. Rosie put on the dress and it fit her perfectly. Then, the Contessa helped her with her makeup and they touched up her hair. Auntie Kate pulled out a beautiful sheer lace scarf that they arranged on her head to cascade down her back. Rosie looked into the mirror and was astonished how in minutes they had transformed the gown into a wedding dress for her. She lifted up her skirt enough to show she was barefoot.

"Just a minute," Contessa swiftly left the room and returned in a minute, holding a pair of ballerina slippers in her hand. "I think this will fit you and with all the dancing, you would be kicking off any high heels you might have worn."

Rosie hugged Contessa and then Auntie Kate, careful not to get hugged to hard by her, "You two just saved the day. Thank you so much."

Auntie Kate just smiled, "Now, let's get things started." She left the room swiftly for a large woman and knocked on all the doors, "Five minutes."

Promptly in five minutes, all the doors opened. They had all been informed that Auntie Kate was in charge.

"When you hear the music start, Mr. and Mrs. O'Ryan, you will lead the family down the stairs, followed by your daughter and her family. There are seats reserved for you. Manny will be there to escort you. Then I want young Daniel and his bride to come down and Cray will show you where to stand, then Jack and his bride will come and stand next to his brother and wife. Any questions?" Hearing none, Auntie Kate once again dressed in the beautiful gold gown with the matching turban went regally down the curved stairway.

The soft strains of music floated up the stairs. "Guess that's our cue," Bob extended his arm to his wife. Together the slowly started down the steps, followed by Deb and her family with Brian holding on to Mira's hand. Then the two married couples holding hands descended the steps.

As before, the room was set up with tables and the buffet on the side wall laden with food. The dancing would be done in the next room.

The two couples stopped at the entryway. It was full of people. Jack's family was seated with Granny and Contessa. Cray and Manny were making sure all was in place and Auntie stood in the front waiting for them.

There were oohs and ahs from the people in the room as the two couples came to stand in front of Auntie Kate.

Auntie Kate raised her hands and brought them down, hushing the assembly of Cajun people.

There was a ringing of bells.

"The bells ring to keep away evil spirits. Peace to us all." Auntie Kate put her hands together and bowed. Auntie Kate looked up at Alice. "Mother, would you please join us?"

Alice looked bewilder, but nodded yes, and Bob rose and escorted her around the table.

Taking out two aprons from her bag, Auntie Kate tied one on Jack and one on Brian. They she removed a pair of scissors and handed them to Alice.

"When you cut the apron strings, this will cut the ties of your sons and they join with their woman in marriage. They are now grown men."

Alice stepped first to her younger son, Daniel and hugged him. Then with a flourish, cut the ties. The apron fell and the crowd clapped.

Then she turned to Jack and hugged him. Turning to the friends asked, "Should I trim his hair first." They all laughed as she snipped through the apron ties.

Again there was a stamping of their feet and laughter.

Alice bowed to Auntie Kate and handed back the scissors.

When Alice was once more seated, Auntie Kate began speaking.

"It is said that there are three ways to be a Cajun: by blood, by marriage, or by the back door. Jack O'Ryan came to us by love and is now in our hearts, along with his bride and his family. Since they have been officially married in their home church in La Crosse, we will do our Cajun one.

It is said the bride should have something old, which is life before marriage.

Something new, this is the new beginning.

Something borrowed, usually from another bride, but we make concessions here there was a twittering of laughter since they all knew about the forgotten dress.

Something blue…now a days it seems like that is a garter around the knee. Once again there was laughter. Cajun people love a good time.

I find it interesting that our Jack gave Rosie an opal when they were engaged. This stone brings emotional, physical and mental harmony. He chose well.

And our new friend, Daniel gave his bride a diamond, which means eternity and courage. And he also chose well."

She beckoned to Manny who carried in two new brooms with a huge blue ribbon around each of them and handed them to Auntie Kate.

"In early times when we Cajun people were in situations when we didn't have the services of a minister like today, it was excepted that a couple could ceremoniously jump the broom together and that was held as a binding marriage until they could be married in a religious ceremony. Not only that, but a good broom is hard to find."

She laid one broom in front of Daniel and Sara, the other in front of Jack and Rosie. "I'll count to three, and then you jump. Ready? One, two, three!" Both couples jumped the broom and no one fell even with the long dresses on.

Little Brian came running over to them, "Me jump too, me jump too. I got married too." He evidently didn't want to miss out on this.

Auntie Kate could see the young man needed this.

"And so you shall Brian. On the count of three, are you ready?"

Brian poised next to the broom, bent his knees and counted with Auntie Kate.

"One, two, three, jump!" Brian jumped over the broom, turned around and got between his new dad and mom.

Daniel picked Brian up and hugged him. "Yes, we are married."

"We will close with a blessing for both couples. 'May God be with you and bless you. May you see your children's children. May you be poor in misfortune, rich in blessings. May you know nothing but Happiness'. Congratulations to the O'Ryans!"

There were cheers and whistles as the crowd stood and clapped.

Both couples bowed to them, smiling from ear to ear.

"And now we eat and then we dance." Auntie Kate motioned for them to go first through the buffet, followed by the family.

On the table were the traditional gumbo, jambalaya, cleaned crawfish heads stuffed with a dressing mixture, corn bread and many side dishes and a whole roasted pig and alligator meat. The aromas were causing all of their stomachs to growl. The spices were pungent with garlic, onion, and veggies. The two brides looking at one another knew what the other was thinking…did you bring breath mints…we have to dance with garlic and onion breathe?

As they traveled down the tables laden with food, they stopped and began laughing at the dessert table. There was a traditional white cake for the brides, and a chocolate cake for the men decorated with a semi and a small truck stop.

After they had all eaten their fill, the band began to play. The married couples first did a promenade around the dance floor then began to dance a waltz; they were joined by the parents who danced with the married couples followed by the family and the Cajun friends. Soon, the men were handing out dollars to dance with the brides, and the ladies doing the same for the men.

Before long the slow music got faster until all types of dancing was keeping the dance floor full of people. At the stroke of midnight, the O'Ryan family had to call it a night. Mira and Katie though tired were still awake, but little Brian had cuddled up next to Granny and with his head in her lap was sound asleep.

As Manny and Clay went to get the vans, Rosie hugged Contessa, "I'll change back into my jeans. Thank you so much for letting me wear your beautiful dress."

"Oh, no. The dress is yours, my gift to you and may every time you wear it you will remember the magic of a Cajun wedding and your bayou family." Contessa smiled at her.

Hugging Contessa again, Rosie whispered, "I never had a sister, I do now."

During the ride back to the big city of New Orleans, those in both vans were busy going over the day's excitements, except for the young ones who were fast asleep.

Jack unlocked the door to their suite at the hotel, picked up Rosie to carry her over the entry and was amazed to find it full of balloons. They started to laugh; this must be one more of Auntie Kate's tricks. He kissed her gently before letting her stand on her own. They stood there locked in each other's arms. Finally, they were officially married by pastor and now the Cajun people. It had been a long, but wonderful day that would never be forgotten.

"I love you Mr.O'Ryan." Rosie kissed him.

"I love you more, Mrs. O'Ryan" Jack returned her kiss.

And so began the married life of Jack and Rosie who after a brief honeymoon would team drive back and forth across the United States. And those experiences are another story.

The End

ABOUT THE AUTHOR

Donna Bryan was born and raised in La Crosse, Wisconsin, a town full of history with the mighty Mississippi River flowing by separating it from Minnesota. The city spreads out into farmland with Granddad Bluff watching over it. Even Mark Twain in *Life on the Mississippi* mentioned Granddad Bluff, from the top where one can see three states.

Donna has also lived in Minnesota and Missouri with her family. Throughout these moves, she has always enjoyed writing articles, worship services, children's stories, and programs.

Most of the *Truck Drivin' Man* came to Donna in the early morning hours and she would get up and type it out before leaving for work. She hopes you enjoy reading the journey of Jack, the truck driver, as much as she did writing it.

More about Donna and her latest writing projects can be found at: **www.DonnaMBryan.com**.

DONNA M. BRYAN

Made in the USA
Lexington, KY
11 December 2016